crossing jordan

adrian fogelin

PEACHTREE
ATLANTA

For my daughter, Josephine Sandberg Faass
With thanks to my husband, Ray Faass, and my agent, Jack Ryan
And to the Wednesday Night Writers—Beverly, Helen, Linda, Noanne,
Richard, and Taylor—thanks for listening.

CP
JR

A Peachtree Junior Publication

Published by
PEACHTREE PUBLISHERS
1700 Chattahoochee Avenue
Atlanta, Georgia 30318-2112

www.peachtree-online.com

Text © 2000 by Adrian Fogelin
Illustrations © 2000 by Suzy Schultz

First trade paperback edition published June 2002

Jacket and cover design by Loraine M. Joyner
Composition by Melanie McMahon Ives

Manufactured in the United States of America

10 9 8 7 (hardcover)
10 9 8 (trade paperback edition)

Library of Congress Cataloging-in-Publication Data

Fogelin, Adrian.
    Crossing Jordan / Adrian Fogelin. -- 1st ed.
      p. cm.
    Summary: Twelve-year-old Cass meets her new African-American neighbor, Jemmie, and despite their families' prejudices, they build a strong friendship around their mutual talent for running and a pact to read Jane Eyre.

    ISBN 13: 978-1-56145-215-6 / ISBN 10: 1-56145-215-7 (hardcover)
    ISBN 13: 978-1-56145-281-1 / ISBN 10: 1-56145-281-5 (trade paperback)

    [1. Neighbors--Fiction. 2. Running--Fiction. 3. Prejudices--Fiction. 4. Afro-Americans--Fiction.] I. Title.
PZ7.F72635 Cr 2000
[Fic]--dc21   99-086978

Please visit the author's website at
adrianfogelin.com

CONTENTS

The Fence

Daddy held out his hand. "Got another one of those nails, String Bean?"

"This fence is awful big," I said, handing him one.

"Good fences make good neighbors," he said, and gave the nail a whack.

"But we won't even be able to *see* the new neighbors with this fence in the way." I pulled my hair back and lifted it to cool my neck. Summer's the worst time to build anything in a hot place like Tallahassee, Florida, but Daddy was determined to finish the fence before the new people moved in.

"If they stay out of our business and we stay out of theirs, we'll get along fine," he said.

The For Sale sign on the house next door had hardly been up a week when Mama told us she'd heard that a black family had bought the old Faircloth place. Daddy brought his fist down on the table and the supper plates jumped. "Place is gonna go downhill," he said.

I didn't know how much further downhill the place could go. The paint was all cracked, and the flower beds were overgrown. Seemed like it was at the bottom of the hill already.

"I'll just have to build a fence," he said.

Mama stopped pouring milk. "Shouldn't we wait and see?" she asked. "They might be nice people."

"Better safe than sorry," he said.

The next night Daddy came home with a huge pile of boards in the back of his pickup.

Mama stepped out of the house with my baby sister, Missy, on her hip. "How much did all that cost, Seth?"

"Not a thing." He laughed and told us it just so happened they were building a pool at the apartment complex where he's the maintenance man, and they had to take down an old fence to do it. "They even paid me to haul it off."

I helped him carry the posts and boards to the side yard, then we spent a whole bunch of evenings with him hammering and me handing him nails and fetching him glasses of iced tea. Now he was hammering the last nail. "There." He lifted his ball cap and wiped his face with his bandanna. "Bet even Michael Jordan couldn't see over that." And he walked off toward the house whistling.

I was just taking a hard look at our new fence, trying to decide whether or not I liked it, when I heard a shout from the street.

"Watch me, Cass!" Cody Floyd was wobbling along on his bike with his older brother, Ben, running behind him.

"Hey, Cody, you're doing good," I called, walking along the fence to the edge of the road. "You take his training wheels off, Ben?"

"Yup." Ben flipped his brown hair out of his eyes and stood for a second with his hands on his hips watching Cody dip and swerve his way down the road. "Don't lean!" He ran and grabbed the seat to keep Cody from falling over.

As I watched Ben chase after his brother, I wondered when he had gotten so cute. He didn't used to be that way, and believe me, I know. I'm an expert on Ben Floyd. We've known each other since we were both babies. Mama has pictures of the two of us in diapers—which I'd like to burn. Even though he's a boy, Ben's always been my best friend. At least until last year. Since then he's been hanging out a lot with a boy named Justin who moved into the neighborhood last summer. I guess it's easier for him. I know it would be easier for me if he was a girl.

And I wish he hadn't gotten cute. Last year other girls started getting all giggly and tongue-tied around him. They were jealous if they saw him talking to me, and the guys teased him. No one would believe that we were just friends.

"Turn, Cody, turn!" Ben jerked his brother's handlebars and the bike came back my way. Ben ran alongside, one hand on the seat. "Your daddy gonna build that fence all the way around?" he called over his shoulder.

"I don't think so."

"That's good." He swooped the bike around again. "Your place'd look like a fort if he did."

"Ben," Cody whined. "I'm getting dizzy going back and forth. I want to go home."

"Okay. See you later," Ben called to me as they streaked by.

Other girls would spend hours on the phone trying to figure out what Ben Floyd meant when he said, "See you later," but like I said, I know him. "See you later" meant see you later.

"Later," Cody repeated. He jingled the bell on his handlebars all the way to their house at the end of the block. He only stopped ringing it when Ben shouted, "Brake, Cody, brake. You're gonna hit the garage!"

Trailing my fingers along the boards of the new fence, I walked back toward the rose of Sharon bush that grew near the edge of our yard. The fence was pretty close to the bush, and it crowded the spot where Ben and me used to play when we were little. We would sit behind the bush, hidden from the house. Sometimes we would throw a blanket over the branches to make a tent. I guess we've outgrown all that now that we're both in middle school.

I still have a chair back there, though, and when my parents and my big sister, Lou Anne, and the baby are all fussing at once, I sit back there, just to get away.

Before we built the fence, I could see the house next door real well. It's the only big house in the neighborhood, and it was built a long, long time ago. It must have been beautiful back then. It has fancy railings and a porch that wraps all the way around. Too bad it hasn't been painted for at least fifty years.

Until March, when she died at ninety-seven, Miss Liz was always out on that porch. She would talk to Ben and me when we were playing by the rose of Sharon bush. After Ben stopped coming over, Miss Liz told me I should come sit up on the porch with her so the two of us could talk "girl to girl." Sitting side by side in the two rockers on the porch, we'd talk. I would tell her about how much I loved to run, and about how I wished I could be pretty like my sister, Lou Anne. Miss Liz would tell me old-timey stories about ice cream socials and hayrides.

"You know, Cass, when I was a girl like you," she'd say, "all this land belonged to my daddy." Then she would sweep her thin, bluish hand through the air, and our house and all the other little houses would disappear. "The buggies would come from that way, up the hill. You'd hear the clomp of hooves on the sand road before you saw them." We'd squint, imagining we could see the horses nodding as they climbed, the buggies swaying, even though we were really only seeing Mr. Martin coming home from the bus stop or Miss Johnette walking her old dog, Gregor.

While we rocked and talked, Miss Liz's fourteen cats—each one named for a Confederate general—took turns napping in her lap or weaving around our ankles. There was General Nathan Bedford Forrest, and General Jubal Early. (We just called him Early—he always got to the food first.) There was also a Jeb Stuart, and a Henry Alexander Wise, and quite a few more I never could keep straight. The biggest one, an orange tomcat, was named General Robert E. Lee. He was always in trouble for sharpening his claws on Miss Liz's chair. After Miss Liz died I took my rocker off the porch and put it in my spot behind the bush. I just know she would've wanted me to have it.

The day of Miss Liz's funeral I felt so bad that Mama let me stay home from school. That's how come I saw Miss Liz's family drive up in a rented moving van. Still dressed in their funeral clothes, they took everything out of her house they thought was valuable, from the porcelain dolls to the rosewood dining table. When they left, Miss Liz's scratched-up rocker was still on the porch.

So were her fourteen cats.

One of the neighbors must have called animal control because a couple of days later they came and netted up thirteen of the fourteen generals. Mr. Barnett, who's home on disability, watched the whole thing, and told me that General Lee squeezed under the porch. The cat catchers were too fat to crawl after him and their nets wouldn't reach, so they left him behind. "Looks like we're down to the last general, Cass," Mr. Barnett said, shaking his head.

After that, the last general yowled at my door twice a day. Once I'd fed him, he'd go back to Miss Liz's porch. No one yelled at him anymore when he sharpened his claws on her rocker.

Sitting in my chair now I was almost smack up against the new fence. Its boards were weathered silver with holes where knots had dropped out. And that's when I discovered it; a knothole at just the right height. If I pressed my knees against the wood and squinched my eye up to it, I could look right into Miss Liz's yard. And I thought, maybe I could do that sometimes; not spying exactly, just looking to see what the new family was up to.

There were other black families in the neighborhood, a couple of streets over, and plenty of black kids in school with me, but I didn't know any of them to talk to. I peered through the hole. All there was to see so far were butterflies in the weeds and General Lee stretching his back in the sunshine.

I wondered when the new family would get there and what they would be like.

CHAPTER TWO

Cat Stealers

The next morning my house seemed like it was set to explode. Upstairs Daddy was pounding the bathroom door and yelling, "Scoot yer boot, Lou Anne, I gotta shave!" Through the kitchen doorway I could see Mama making coffee, carrying the baby on her hip, and packing Daddy's lunch all at the same time. "Come eat your breakfast," she called to Daddy over Missy's crying. "Lou Ann'll be out by the time you're done."

Me, I was sitting on the staircase in the middle of the shouting, putting on my socks and sneakers for a quick getaway.

I dashed into the kitchen. "Bye, Mama." I kissed her cheek, then ran out the front door. The spring on the screen door twanged, and the door slammed behind me.

Outside, it was still cool, and it was quiet. I walked past the end of the fence and looked back at Miss Liz's house. General Lee was walking along the top of the porch railing. "I'll feed you when I get back," I called. He rubbed his face on a column. I wondered if the new people had any kids. I guess it wouldn't matter if they did. Daddy wouldn't want me hanging out with them.

The air felt silky on my bare legs as I began to jog. Halfway down the block the Cortezes' dogs, Fran and Blackie, started running with me. A couple times a year Mr. Cortez has to go get them back from the pound, which makes him mad because it's expensive, but as soon as he opens his car door they're off again, running. Except for the times when they're being thrown in the back of the dog-catcher's truck, Fran and Blackie own the neighborhood.

The brick front of Monroe Middle School looked pink in the morning sun as the dogs and me trotted up. Closed for the summer, the school was dark, except for the safety light over the front door, which I knew would turn itself out at exactly seven-thirty. We jogged across the basketball court. Sometimes while I did my run, Ben would be out there, shooting baskets with his new friend Justin. It wasn't much of a contest, Justin was such a shrimp. But today the court was empty.

I sat down in the damp grass by the track to stretch. The dogs flopped down beside me. When I told them, "You two stay," they cocked their ears like they understood.

Quickly I opened the gate and stepped onto the track. I stood still a minute, then leaned forward, about to run. A breeze blew my hair back and I smelled the dry red dirt.

I was in the third grade when I found out I was fast. It was field day, and everyone was competing in high jump and long jump, in throwing contests, and in races. I was still short in the third grade. I didn't do too well in the jumps. When it was my turn with the softball Ben said I threw like a girl.

Then we lined up for the four-hundred-meter dash.

"On your mark, get set, go!"

When I started running, a funny thing happened. I passed all the girls, and then I passed the boys—even Ben. As I crossed the finish line I was all by myself. When Ben caught up he kept saying it was a miracle, but I could tell he was proud of me. I still have the certificate I got for winning that race. I'll always remember that day. That was the day I found out what was special about me, that I could run. Now everybody says, "Cass Bodine? She's the girl who runs."

This year I'll be in the seventh grade, so I can join the track team. Then, look out! I bet I'll win sometimes, even against eighth and ninth graders. But winning isn't the important thing. Running's the important thing. I just love to run.

I looked at the track and said to myself, ready, set, go! Then I took off. As I rushed by, the tree beside the track and the two dogs lying underneath it blurred. I must've been a blur to Fran and Blackie too, I was moving so fast. I wasn't tired yet, or too hot. It seemed as if I was still picking up speed; like if I pushed a little harder I would reach escape velocity. Running that fast, all the fussing back at the house faded until there was no sound in the whole world but the double-time rhythm of my own flying feet.

∼

I made Lou Anne and me grilled cheese sandwiches for lunch. She said that next time they could use more cheese, and I told her that next time she could make her own, then I took my glass of iced tea and went outside.

I was sitting in my chair by the fence watching the glass sweat and wishing Ben would forget he wasn't my best friend anymore and come over, when I heard a racket from the other side of the fence. I put my eye up to the knothole. The pickup that had pulled into Miss Liz's yard said Lewis Painting, Interior/Exterior, No Job Too Small on its door. It was loaded with beds and dressers and boxes. The brakes squawked and all that furniture rocked. The two men in the back had to grab things to keep them from falling out of the truck. Their arm muscles were smooth and shiny as melons.

They laughed. When the truck came to a full stop, one of them opened a can of beer. The other one lit a cigarette. The driver, a skinny old lady with a straw hat shoved down tight on her head, climbed down from the cab and shook her finger. "Y'all can party on your own time. We got stuff to move."

The two men shrugged at each other and started carrying boxes inside.

A pretty, younger woman in a pale blue dress slid out of the truck, then walked around the passenger side and lifted a baby out of a safety seat. "I don't believe this," she said, hugging the baby and glaring at Daddy's fence. "I'll just have to call zoning and see if they got a permit."

The old lady quit bossing and put a hand on the younger woman's arm. "Now, Leona, honey, let it go. Like Jesus says, turn the other cheek. Love thy neighbor."

"I'm sorry. I can't love a bunch of crackers who put up a fence soon as they hear a black family is moving in next door." The younger woman pushed her damp bangs back off her forehead and frowned.

The old lady shook her head. "Jesus never said it'd be easy, child." Then, in a big, loud voice that seemed to be meant for us crackers on the other side of the fence she said, "Me, I like a big old fence. Gives me something to grow my gourds up against."

I heard the passenger door slam and a girl about my age came around the truck. Lucky she was real skinny or they never would've fit everyone in the front of the pickup.

"Take a look at this," the woman in the blue dress said to her. "This is what bigotry looks like."

I pulled back quick, afraid they'd see me. But I didn't want to miss anything, so I put my other eye up to the hole. The girl had only looked at Daddy's fence for a second before the old lady put a hand on the back of her neck and turned her around. "Let her make up her own mind about all that, Leona. See that house?" she asked the girl. "It's all ours. That's what's important."

The girl climbed the front steps and lifted Robert E. Lee out of Miss Liz's chair, then she sat down with the cat in her lap. "Look what I found, Nana Grace." She stretched her long legs out and rocked. Her skin was as dark as black coffee. Gold hoops sparkled in her pierced ears. I wanted pierced ears in the worst way, but Daddy had put his foot down. "Only ethnics pierce their ears," he said.

The girl giggled. The general was rubbing his whiskers against her face. "Looks like we got us a cat!"

I almost shouted, "Put the general down. He's Miss Liz's cat." Then I remembered I was spying.

A loud crash sounded from inside and the old lady, Nana Grace, marched her red tennis shoes up the steps, yelling, "Do I have to knock heads?"

When the furniture and boxes were all inside the house, she drove away with the two men in the back of the truck. She came back without them.

~

"The new neighbors are two women, a baby, and a girl," I reported at the supper table.

"Not surprised," Daddy said, spooning peas onto his plate. "With them, the men run off. The women take care of the kids."

"Now, Seth...." Mama raised her eyebrows and put her hand on top of his. She was afraid to come out and say it, but she didn't like that kind of talk.

"Well, it's true," he said, and pulled his hand away.

That night, I put out a dish of food for General Lee but he didn't come. I wondered if Daddy was right. Those people hadn't been in the neighborhood one day, and already they'd stolen a cat.

CHAPTER THREE

The Girl on the Other Side of the Fence

The next morning, after I had run at the track, I made a big bowl of chicken potato salad. Even though I'm younger than Lou Anne, cooking supper is my summer job. I don't mind. First, I like to cook, and second, if Lou Anne did it we'd all starve. Lou Anne could mess up buttering toast.

Between peeling the potatoes, boiling the potatoes and the chicken, taking off the chicken skin, chopping the meat, making sure all the bones are out, dicing the celery, and adding the mayonnaise, salt, and pepper, making chicken potato salad is a big job. Especially with no help from Lou Anne.

I knew that in the evening Mama would put my salad and some napkins and plastic forks and a jar of iced tea in a basket and we'd go to Wakulla Springs to swim. After all that chopping and boiling, I could hardly wait.

I went up to the room I shared with Lou Anne to change my sweaty shirt. "Cass..." she whined as soon as I walked in, "can't you see I'm on the phone?"

"So?"

Lou Anne was always on the phone, talking to her boyfriend, Andy, or else talking to her girlfriend, Carey, about Andy. Now she was sprawled on her bed, her long, blond hair hanging down over the edge, the phone clamped to her ear. "Please...I need some privacy."

"I'm on my own side," I said, pointing at the old red belt Lou Anne had stretched out on the floor between our beds.

"Cass, Missy's asleep. It's my only chance to talk." It was Lou Anne's summer job to mind the baby. "Pretty please, go away." She rolled her eyes toward the door.

"Okay, okay." I turned to the wall and changed my T-shirt quick, then I picked up my book and left.

When I got to my spot behind the rose of Sharon I just sat with the heavy old book in my lap. It was called *Jane Eyre* and it smelled musty, like a sweater from a bottom drawer. Miss Liz gave it to me when I told her I was lonely because Ben didn't spend time with me anymore. "A book can be such a good friend," she said. "This one was my favorite when I was your age."

Now that she was dead, I had to read it.

So far I had only made it to page five.

As I glanced down at the swarm of tiny words, a bee landed on the open book. It walked across page five, down into the ditch, then up page four before it flew away. I tried to concentrate on the words, but the leather cover was making my knees sweat.

Between the bush and the fence, I could see the street. Ben and Justin were walking by. Justin was trying to show Ben how he could dribble a basketball and walk backwards at the same time. If it had been just Ben by himself, he'd have come over to talk to me. Justin always made these stupid kissing sounds when Ben talked to me.

I pretended like I didn't see them. I looked down at the book in my lap and read, "John had not much affection for his mother and sisters and an antipathy to me."

Antipathy? That was the problem with *Jane Eyre*. It was chock-full of words like "antipathy." Miss Liz must have known what they meant. When she was young, people probably used words like "antipathy" all the time. I bet they had them on their spelling lists. Since then, though, people have forgotten all about them.

I was still struggling with the first paragraph on page six when I heard the screen door slam at Miss Liz's house. Two pairs of feet thumped down the porch steps, then *shush*ed across the grass.

"Set the baby down on this blanket, child, he's ready to nap." I recognized Nana Grace's gritty voice. They were right there, inches away. I felt the skin on the back of my neck prickle. "Hand me that screwdriver so I can pry this lid off."

Pry the lid off what?

"Hope this stuff is still good," Nana Grace muttered. "Been a while. Give it a stir and see."

"It's thick," the girl said, "but not too bad."

Slap-slap, slap-slap, was the sound from the other side of the fence. "Now, ain't that a pretty color?" Nana Grace asked. "Might just be a leftover from one of your daddy's jobs, but I couldn't've picked a better color myself."

I put my eye up to the knothole. They were painting their side of Daddy's fence canary yellow. They were off to one side, but sometimes I could see the paint bucket and little bits of the girl and her grandmother: a flash of dark skin, a patch of pink T-shirt, or the checked pattern of Nana Grace's housedress.

After the slapping sound had gone on for a while, Nana Grace began to sing. "I am a poor...wayfarin' stranger...just travelin' through...this world of woe."

"Nana...." The girl sounded like I do when Lou Anne embarrasses me. Just like Lou Anne, though, Nana Grace paid no mind. She went right on singing.

When she got to the chorus the girl began to sing too. She didn't sound like she was willing, more like she couldn't help it. The grandmother's voice was low and kind of tired. It flowed like some sluggish old summertime river, carrying the girl's high voice along like a floating leaf. I tipped my chair back against the fence and listened. It sounded like church, but lonelier with just the two voices. "I'm only crossing...over Jordan, I'm only going...over home," they sang.

After a while the singing petered out and all I could hear was the slap of their paintbrushes. "I might just rest my eyes awhile," Nana Grace said. "Mind Artie, okay?"

"Yes, Nana."

One pair of feet thumped back up the steps.

I could tell when Artie woke up because the girl started fussing at him. "Don't put that bug in your mouth, Artie." I heard a little slapping sound as the girl brushed the baby's hands off, then a minute later I heard, "What did you put in your mouth now? Come on, bad boy, open up." Their baby seemed like a lot more work than ours, maybe because he could crawl. I squinched my eye up to the knothole and watched. Every five seconds the girl had to lay her brush down and chase after the baby. Then she'd pick him up under the arms and lug him to a different spot. Each time Artie'd find something new to stick in his mouth.

The girl held her hand out. "Come on, spit it," she said, but he wouldn't. She squeezed his fat cheeks and out popped a rock. "Bad boy." To keep the baby out of trouble, she hefted him up on her hip. It took both hands under Artie's butt to hold him up. Her hip was too small to make a good shelf.

While she stood there, I had my first close-up view. She was real skinny and tall like me. Her long legs seemed to start at the ground and end at her ears. On each of her braids was a bunch of blue beads that rattled when she turned her head. She had a sun dangling from one ear, a moon from the other.

All of a sudden she quit telling Artie what a bad boy he was and stuck her lip out until I could see the pink inside of it. "Don't think I don't see your big old blue eye," she said. I jerked my head back. "Bet you're some snotty boy spying on me." Next thing I knew, a brown eye was looking back at me through the hole in the fence.

The brown eye looked and looked. "That all you got over there?" the girl said at last. "Just a run-down old house, a coupla trees, and an old rockin' chair?"

"What'd you expect?"

"I dunno. Guess I thought there'd be all kinds of stuff." The brown eye blinked. "My mother says y'all figured you had a black family movin' in next door and you were bound to get robbed. That's why you put up this fence, isn't it?"

I couldn't think of anything to say quick, so I blurted the truth. "My father says it's just better not to mix."

"You agree?"

I didn't know whether I did or not. "You got a name?" I asked.

"Jemmeal Constance Lewis. Jemmie for short. You?"

"Catherine Margaret Bodine. Cass." I thought about her long, skinny legs. "Do you like to run?"

"Run? Girl, I don't run, I fly. Can't nobody beat me."

"Bet I could."

The brown eye disappeared. I heard a whoop of laughter from the other side of the fence. "Dream on, girl. I would leave you so far behind, you'd be stuck in the middle of last week." The words came over the fence in a rush. "I would leave you so far back you'd need a map to find me." She must've set Artie down because I heard her tell him to be good or else, then—*bing*— the brown eye was back, and she was telling me to get myself kind of centered so she could look me over. I felt funny, but I stood up like she said. The eyeball looked me up and down. "Got some long legs on you," the girl conceded. "Wouldn't do you no good, though. I'd still beat you."

"Would not," I said.

"Would too," she said.

"Jemmie!" Nana Grace called from the porch. "Your head in the clouds? Artie's eatin' grass again."

"Sorry, Nana." Before she picked the baby back up she hissed, "Could too beat you."

"You think so? Meet me at the school, seven-thirty tomorrow morning." I know she heard me, but she didn't answer because just then the Lewis Painting truck pulled into the driveway. Its driver door opened and out stepped the woman who had called us crackers: Jemmie's mother. She was wearing white pants with a sharp crease pressed into them. She had a name tag pinned to her blue flowered top. She took the baby out of Jemmie's arms and gave Jemmie a kiss.

Nana Grace called down from the front porch, "How was your day, Leona?" She was sitting in Miss Liz's rocker with a towel over her shoulder and General Lee in her lap.

"Not so good," she answered, carrying Artie up the steps. "We lost that baby with the hole in his heart."

"I'm so sorry." Nana Grace covered her own heart with her hand. "You did what you could. He's with Jesus now."

Jemmie went up the porch steps and they all went inside, but in a minute Jemmie came back out and picked up the general. "Come on, Poppy," she said. She stood there for a moment more, gazing over at the fence, then she pointed at herself and held up one finger. I'm number one, she was saying. Hugging the cat, she went back inside.

I couldn't wait to beat the pants off her.

◊

Lou Anne was lying on a towel beside the blue water of Wakulla Springs. "Oil my back, wouldya, Cass?"

"It'll be dark in another hour, Lou."

"Oh, do it anyway," she said, gathering her hair up and draping it to the side. Lou Anne would've made a good princess. She's pretty and blond and she likes people to do stuff for her.

I squirted lotion into my palm. "I think the new lady is a nurse, Mama," I said, rubbing the oil on Lou Anne.

My mother grabbed the baby's ankles, lifted her butt, and scooted a fresh diaper under her. "That's nice," she said. I could tell she wasn't really listening.

Lou Anne lifted a shoulder. "You missed a spot, Cass."

"Like it matters...." I gave her back a slap.

She tried to grab my ankle, but I sprinted to the water and plunged in. Right away I felt my skin get goose-bumpy. Summer or winter, the water bubbling out of the ground at the spring is always the same temperature. Freezing. It'll make your scalp pucker and turn your lips blue.

As I came up I heard a couple of boys up on the diving tower. "Go on, you first, D. J., I double dare you." Then they both hollered and jumped together.

Mama waded in. She was wearing the old pink swimsuit she's had as long as I can remember. She'll have it forever; she never gets it wet. She stood knee-deep in the icy spring and swished Missy's feet in the water. The baby pulled them up.

I swam over to where my father was floating on his back. His belly poked out of the water, white like a dead fish. He'd been mowing lawns all day. Bet the cold felt good to him.

I put my feet down and grabbed his hand. "I'm gonna take you for a ride," I said, and began towing him slowly through the water.

He opened one eye. "Get back from the rope, Cass. I don't want to be gator bait."

"Sorry, Daddy." I pulled him the other way.

The spring has so much water that it turns into a wide river. Alligators like to sun themselves on its banks. They look lazy, but they can be awful fast. Once in a while they drag a swimmer to the bottom and drown him. It happened right here at Wakulla a few years ago. A college kid swam out past the rope and a bull gator got him.

"Daddy, what makes the gators stay on their side of the rope?" I asked, towing him in a big circle.

"Don't know, but they do. As long as we stay on our side, we're safe."

That made me think about the fence. I had stayed on our side, but I had talked to Jemmie Lewis. I had even asked her to meet me somewhere. I knew I should tell my parents about it. Mama probably wouldn't mind, but Daddy would. I thought maybe I could tell him after I beat her at the track.

CHAPTER FOUR

You Think You're Fast?

She wasn't coming. I should've known. It was way past 7:30. The safety light over the school door had been out a long time and I had stretched until I was as loose as an old rubber band.

The gate creaked as I opened it and stepped onto the track. I started to run.

I was halfway around when the gate creaked again. "All right," called a voice, "I'll give you a head start."

"I don't need one." I slowed until Jemmie Lewis pulled up next to me. I took a sidelong glance at her. "Thought you chickened."

"I ain't afraid of you." Jemmie Lewis had baggy shorts and a tank top on. Her bare arms were real skinny. Skinny as mine.

We were even with the gate when she said, "Race you back to here. Bye." And she shot off, pumping her skinny arms. I guess she thought she'd leave me in the dust, but I ran right along with her. Our strides were identical. Our knees and elbows rose and fell together.

She wasn't trying for that.

I wasn't either.

Each of us was trying our hardest to pull ahead. In science class last year we learned that some stars revolve around each other, caught in each other's gravity. We were like that, caught, and neither one of us could break away.

We were cool for a second as we ran through the shadow of the pecan tree, then we were back in the scorching sun. Jemmie was breathing through her mouth. I could see her neck muscles strain as we neared the gate. I blinked the sweat out of my eyes. As we passed the gate, our shoulders were almost touching.

She rolled her eyes my way to see if I was going to stop. I did the same. Neither one of us even slowed. We went around again.

"Ya tired?" she asked as we passed the gate for the second time.

Even though I felt like someone had punched a hole in my chest, I said, "No." To show her I wasn't, I put on a burst of speed and got a couple of feet ahead of her.

"Me neither." She caught back up.

After a while, I stopped thinking and just listened to the dull blows of our sneakers on the track. By then I felt like I had pounded my legs into the clay up to my knees and that for each step I had to lift my foot out of a deep hole.

When we'd started, her shoulders had been pinned back as if she was thrusting her chest out to break a tape at the finish line. I noticed that they sagged now. It didn't matter what her mouth had to say about it, she was tired too.

She pulled a small envelope out of the pocket of her shorts and tore the top with her teeth. She tipped her head back and shook some sparkly powder onto her tongue.

Daddy had a friend who was shot by a black teenager in a liquor store holdup. "The kid was high as a kite," Daddy said. "A lot of them get hooked on drugs."

Jemmie Lewis was folding the envelope top as she ran, not slowing down a bit.

"What is that?" I demanded.

"This? Foaming Fizz Powder. Check it out." She passed me the packet. Mr. Foamy, a goofy smiling bubble, was on the front. I tried some. The powder foamed and hissed. Crackly noises burst inside my head. Foaming Fizz Powder tasted like a handful of lemon-coated rusty nails. It was good.

Mr. Foamy kept us going for a while, but what we really needed was water.

"You know," Jemmie said, "my mother says...you can get...the heat prostration if you...exercise in this kind of weather."

"What's that?"

"It's when you…get so heated up, you drop over."

"Dead?"

"Sometimes."

"I don't believe that," I said, but suddenly I felt kind of weak.

"You better believe it. My mother's a nurse. She sees it all the time…over at the hospital, folks who just…keeled flat over on their faces."

I could hear a loud buzz in my head. Maybe that was what you heard right before you keeled over. I licked my lips and tasted salt. "Listen," I said. "I don't want to drop over dead."

"And you think I do?" Beads of sweat ran down her neck.

"How about if we…call it a tie. You didn't win. I didn't win. Okay?"

She looked at me hard to be sure it wasn't a trick. "Okay."

Together, we ran off the track and collapsed under the pecan tree.

As the grass pricked me through my T-shirt I saw black stars. The buzz in my head became a roar. We were both breathing like we'd been underwater for minutes. Finally, Jemmie sat up, lifted the hem of her shirt to blot her face, and said, "Girl, you are fast."

"You're fast too," I admitted, sitting up.

She roped her arms around her bent knees. "No doubt about that," she said, staring off at the school. While she studied Monroe Middle, I studied her. Daddy said he couldn't tell black people apart. They all have the same big lips, he said, the same dark eyes with the whites all around. They all look alike.

Not Jemmie Lewis. For one thing, she had an extra-long neck, and her ears were small and pink, like seashells. Today a pair of howling coyote earrings dangled from her earlobes. Even though her skin was dark all over, she had an even darker spot just below the corner of her left eye. An angel kiss, Mama would have called it. That's what she calls birthmarks.

Jemmie picked up a pebble and tossed and caught it. "I'll be going to this school. Is it okay?"

"I guess. What grade?"

"Seventh."

"Me too."

She stood up and dusted her shorts off. "I gotta go home now." She walked a couple of steps, then looked back at me. "Better rest up, girl. I mean to whip your butt."

"You can try."

She pointed a finger at me. "Tomorrow," she said. "Same time. Same place." Then she grinned.

I grinned back. "I'll be here."

She was walking by the basketball court when Ben came from the other direction, dribbling the ball on the sidewalk. "Hey," he said, "didn't you just move into the Faircloth house?"

"Uh-huh."

"You wouldn't happen to have a brother who plays basketball, would you?" I guess he was hoping for a little more competition than Justin could give him.

"My brother's eleven months old." She stood with her feet wide apart, her hips thrust forward. "But I shoot hoops."

"Nah," said Ben, flipping his hair out of his eyes. "I don't play with girls."

"No?" She knocked the ball out of his hands, dribbled it between her legs, then popped it back at him. "I can see why."

~

Jemmie and Nana Grace spent the afternoon on the other side of the fence, digging. I could hear the soil making scratchy noises against their shovels. After they'd been shoveling a while Nana Grace said, "Pile them pebbles here, child. We can use 'em to edge the garden."

Then later she said, "My old back don't feel like bending, Jemmie. You can plant 'em. Poke yer finger in the dirt up to the first knuckle and drop the seed in. Cover it good, and pat it down. That's all there is to it."

From inside our house I could hear Missy crying and crying.

"Lord," Nana Grace said, "don't nobody mind that baby over there? Poor little thing."

That made me mad. Lou Anne was supposed to be taking care of Missy, but the crying went on and on and Nana Grace said, "Lord, don't them people know enough to pick up a crying baby?"

I stomped into the house and there was Lou Anne, eating a big bowl of peach ice cream with her curtain of blond hair hung over the back of the sofa and the TV on.

"Are you deaf?" I asked.

"Oh, Cass, I've been trying to get her to nap for an hour. Mama says that sometimes you just have to let her cry."

I climbed the stairs and went into my parents' room. Missy had gotten herself all scrunched up against the bars of her crib. Her fuzz of reddish hair was stuck to her scalp. Lou Anne had dressed her in a hot flannel sleeper. "You poor little thing." I lifted her out and laid her on the bed. When I took off the sleeper her skin was pink and splotchy. I powdered her all over, even in the folds in her arms and under her chin. Then I picked her up and carried her down the stairs to the living room.

Lou Anne was polishing her toenails with one hand and holding the phone with the other. The TV was blabbing. I don't think she even noticed I had the baby with me when I left the house.

I showed Missy the little windmill Daddy had put on the front lawn. But she kept trying to grab the blades, so I showed her the mailbox instead. She liked watching me open and close it.

I hoped that Jemmie Lewis was looking through the hole in the fence. I wasn't sure she could see me with the bush in the way, but if she could, she'd see I knew how to take care of a baby as good as she did.

We were still playing with the mailbox when Mrs. Henry's beat-up Cadillac turned onto Magnolia Way. Mama was sitting beside Mrs. Henry, and she was laughing. They stopped in the road in front of the house. "Thanks for the lift, Beth," Mama said, giving Mrs. Henry's arm a pat and climbing out. Mama isn't thin and trim like Jemmie's mother and she doesn't wear a crisp, pressed uniform. She's plump with freckled pink skin, and she wears stretch slacks and a polyester blouse to work. She does the cooking and the housekeeping at the children's shelter. Sometimes she comes home with stains all down the front of her blouse, especially on spaghetti day.

She smiled when she saw me. "Oh Cass, guess what I have?" She didn't give me a chance to guess before she reached into the tote bag hanging off her arm and pulled out the surprise. Magazines.

People bring their old magazines to the shelter for the kids to look at. When they get tired of them, Mama brings them home to us. "Are they fashion magazines for Lou?" I asked.

"No, these are just for you." She held them out to me and I could see the runner on one of the covers.

"Oh, Mama!" We juggled the baby and the magazines, trading off. "Thank you." There were three magazines, and they were all about running. I hugged them to my chest.

Mama beamed. "I snatched them right up for you. I knew you'd like them." Mama had never actually seen me run, but she knew how much I loved it because I talked about it all the time.

Now she settled baby Missy on her hip and put her free arm around my neck. "I guess Lou Anne's inside talking to that Andy, if you have the baby." She sighed. "Lord knows I love her, but that sister of yours is lazy as a cat."

When we walked into the living room my sister was curled up on the couch, asleep. "Pretty as an angel," Mama whispered.

"She looks like she's about to drool."

"Don't be jealous, Cass. Each of you girls has gifts. Lou Anne's pretty, but you're pretty too in your own way, and you're good at school," she said, rushing ahead, "and you can run. Your sister can't do that."

I *can* run. I ducked my head and gave the running magazines a quick sniff, just to see what they smelled like.

"Hi, Mama." Lou Anne yawned and stretched. "What's for supper, Cass?"

"Burgers and macaroni salad," I said.

"Macaroni salad again?"

"Cass makes wonderful macaroni salad," Mama told her.

After supper, while everyone else watched TV, I sat on my bed and spread the three running magazines out in a fan. I flipped through each of them slowly, looking at the pictures of runners on tracks and runners crossing fields and runners jogging straight up mountain roads. If I read them slow I could make them last a long time, so I decided to read only one article before putting them away for the night.

I flipped past the one about buying the perfect sports bra. I could read that one later—like in a couple of years.

I flipped by an article about the Boston Marathon.

Then I came to one about The Zone. I settled back and read. It seemed like The Zone was a place in your head that you had to find to run your best.

"The Zone," I said to the empty room, and felt a surge of power.

CHAPTER FIVE

Jemmie and Jane
and Another Tie

Jemmie and me met the next morning for a rematch.

We did straddle stretches in the grass with the Cortezes' dogs lying beside us. "Sit-ups next," Jemmie said.

I felt a strange coldness, as if I was about to do something wrong. "You want to lock feet?" I asked. "It makes it easier."

"Sure."

I could feel her bony ankles through my socks. Her black skin and my white skin were right together.

She was looking at our side-by-side skin too. "You sure got a lot of freckles," she said.

"My mother's Irish. I mean, she's an American, but her family came from Ireland a long time ago."

We lay on our backs. "Why'd they come over here?" she asked.

"They were hungry. There was a disease that killed all their potatoes, which is what they ate over there, mostly." I felt a hard pull on my ankles as she did her first sit-up. "Why'd your folks come?" I asked, sitting up as she lay back down.

"They didn't come. They were tied up and brought."

I didn't know what to say so I kept quiet.

After the sit-ups, we ran four races. I tried to find The Zone, but I think I missed it. Jemmie said she won two and I won two. I kept telling her that one of mine was really a tie, so she was the winner. "We'll settle it tomorrow," she said.

And then it was time to go. It would have been nice to walk together, but we didn't. She went first. I followed about a block behind her with the Cortezes' dogs trotting back and forth between us. One time I almost shouted something to her. Then I remembered, we weren't supposed to know each other.

When I stopped to pick flowers in a vacant lot, Jemmie and the dogs went on without me. The graveyard where Miss Liz is buried is on the way home from the school. I bring her wildflowers all the time.

Speckles of light fell through the leaves of the tree above her grave. "Hi, Miss Liz. Guess what? There are some new people in your house," I said, arranging the flowers in the pickle jar I had put on top of her stone. "They're black. They seem pretty nice. They're feeding General Lee now. They call him Poppy, but he doesn't seem to mind."

Miss Liz's grave was mostly bare dirt. Daddy had given me some grass seed to sprinkle on it, but it didn't come up. "I'm saving my allowance to get you a plant," I told her. I felt bad. Since the funeral had blown over, no one but me had brought Miss Liz a single flower.

"Well, I gotta go. See you tomorrow maybe." A little breeze lifted the hair on the back of my head, like Miss Liz was saying good-bye. I started to go, then turned and walked backwards. "Did I tell you the new family has a daughter who likes to run?"

∼

When I got home, Lou Anne was putting on her favorite peach lipstick. "You going somewhere?" I asked.

"Just down to the USA store." She tossed her hair back over her shoulders and picked up Missy. "We're out of milk."

"And Andy Thompson's going on his morning break in fifteen minutes."

"So?" Lou Anne acted like it didn't mean a thing to her. "We need some milk, is all."

"Let me take a shower and I'll walk with you."

Lou Anne's eyes made a desperate dart to the clock. "We're ready to go now."

"We must need that milk awful bad," I teased as I put a hat on the baby's head. I didn't want the sun giving Missy the heat prostration just because Lou Anne was too busy thinking about Andy Thompson to cover her head.

My sister lit out of the house with the baby bouncing on her hip. She'd have to walk quick to make it in fifteen minutes. "It's a good thing Andy Thompson's working this summer," I called after her, "otherwise you wouldn't get any exercise at all, Lou Anne." While she was gone I read "The Seven Secrets of Successful Runners." I thought maybe I'd give Jemmie my magazines to read when I was done, as long as she promised to give them back.

~

When Lou Anne came back to the house, she was licking a Popsicle Andy had given her. She looked at the lunch I'd put on the table. "I'll just skip lunch, Cass. I'm on a diet."

"A Popsicle diet?"

I ate as much as I could and put the rest in the refrigerator.

After, we watched a couple of talk shows. "Let me get that hair off your neck," Lou Anne said. She made me a French braid while we watched TV, then handed me a mirror. "Pretty?" she asked.

I nodded.

I still had time before I had to fix supper. I could've read "Tricks and Tips to Beat the Running Blahs," but I was already halfway through my first magazine and I didn't want to finish it too soon. I took *Jane Eyre* outside to my chair instead.

I had barely found my place when I heard, "Like your hair." Jemmie was peeking through the hole in the fence. "What are ya reading?"

"A dumb old book called *Jane Eyre*."

"If it's so dumb, how come you're reading it?"

"Miss Liz gave it to me."

"She the old lady who used to live in my house?"

"*Her* house. Her daddy built it. She lived in it her whole life. It will always be her house."

When she didn't answer right back I wondered if I'd hurt her feelings.

"Sounds like you liked her," she said at last.

"I did. We were friends. That's why I have to read this stupid book. It was her dying wish."

"What page you up to?"

"Eleven."

"Outta how many?"

I turned to the back of the book and sighed. "Four hundred and thirty-three."

She was quiet for a second. "Why don't we take turns reading it to each other?"

I thought about the two of us sitting together like Ben and me used to do. But Daddy wouldn't like it, that was for sure. "You can't come over here," I said.

"Who said anything about that? We can pass it back and forth."

"Well, I guess that's all right."

Jemmie got herself a chair and set it near the knothole. "Meet ya at the end of the fence," she said. We walked down there. One skinny arm reached around to my side. Her fingers closed on the cover. "Got it."

We went back to our chairs. Then, even though I told her she wouldn't miss a thing by starting on eleven, she went right back to page one. "'There was no possibility of taking a walk that day,'" she began. "'We had been wandering, indeed, in the leafless shrubbery an hour in the morning... ' How old's this book, anyway?" I heard her flip the pages back. "Eighteen forty-seven," she said. "Older than God."

"I told you you wouldn't like it. It's really hard."

"Who said I didn't like it? And it's not that hard."

It seemed like Jemmie had to prove that she was good at everything; not just running, but basketball, reading, everything. Jemmie wasn't afraid to take on anybody: not me, or Ben, or even *Jane Eyre*.

I tipped my chair back and listened. Jemmie was a good reader, but I could tell, even though she wouldn't admit it, that she didn't know what half the words meant either. I asked her about "antipathy" when she got to it. "I'll tell you later," she said, and went right on reading.

After a while the story got better. Jane was an orphan. Nobody really wanted her, and the Reeds—who, for some reason, were stuck with her—were mean to her all the time. They locked Jane in the very room where old Mr. Reed had died—which was interesting in a creepy kind of way.

We changed readers every couple of pages. Each time, just an arm and the book would come around the end of the fence. Still, it made me nervous. Lou Anne and Nana Grace were inside our houses. All they had to do was look out and they'd see us. For a while, though, we didn't get caught.

Chocolate Milk

We went along fine for a week or so. Mornings, we ran at the school. Sometimes I won, sometimes Jemmie did. She was better at the shorter distances, so she won most of the sprints. But the longer distances were mine. I would run and run until she just stopped, put her hands on her hips, and shook her head. "Who put the quarter in you, girl?" she'd say.

We practiced passing each other and keeping each other from passing. Jemmie was real good at keeping me from passing. She'd squeeze over just when I was set to go. Seemed like she could read my mind.

One morning we found a stick under the pecan tree and began running relays. Neither of us had ever run a relay before. Sometimes we handed the stick off to each other, sometimes we tossed it back and forth as we ran. Sometimes we trotted along, each of us holding an end. We made it up as we went along.

After a while it seemed like we weren't Cass and Jemmie when we ran. We were more like two parts of one machine.

One morning after a hard run we were lying in the shade by the track. Jemmie had her head against Fran and I had mine on Blackie. "You know," I said, "we can join the track team at school."

Jemmie rolled onto her belly and propped up her chin with her hands. "We're already a team," she said. "We're Chocolate Milk."

"Chocolate Milk?" My head was going up and down as Blackie breathed.

"That's us. And we're gonna blow everyone away. Girl, those other teams won't know what hit 'em when Chocolate Milk comes to town." She got excited as she described it to me. "Say Monroe Middle has an away meet. We'll share a seat on the bus, naturally."

If Daddy caught me sharing a seat with a black girl he would have a fit, but I didn't tell Jemmie. School was still far away.

"When Chocolate Milk climbs off the bus," Jemmie said, "the other runners will take one look and get all weak and crumbly round the knees because they've heard about us."

I reached behind my head to scratch Blackie. "How'd they hear?"

"Read about us in the paper." She thought for a minute, then told me all the ways we would win. Sometimes by a nose, sometimes by a mile. But however we did it, it was always Chocolate Milk in the lead, Chocolate Milk the winner!

Pretty soon I got so excited, I stood back up. "Come on, Jemmie, let's traverse." Traverse was one of our *Jane Eyre* words. Jane Eyre didn't walk or run when she wanted to get somewhere. She traversed.

Traverse wasn't the only word we learned from *Jane Eyre*. When we hit a word we didn't know Jemmie would look it up in her mother's dictionary and report back. Of course, the first one she looked up was antipathy. "Ooh, girl, let me tell you. When it says Master Reed viewed Jane with antipathy, it means he hated her, and then some."

Preternatural was another one. Jane's days were not just long, they were preternaturally long.

Of course, once we had gone to all the trouble of looking the words up we had to use them. "Girl," Jemmie said after we'd been pounding the track a while, "does this race seem preternaturally long to you?"

"Not for Chocolate Milk," I said, running faster. "Chocolate Milk traverses every preternaturally long race in record time."

"That's right," Jemmie crowed, putting on a burst of speed herself. "When Chocolate Milk comes to town, the other team views them with *an*tipathy."

~

Each afternoon while Nana Grace napped and Missy napped and Lou Anne sat on the sofa watching soaps and talk shows, Jemmie and me would cock our two chairs back against the fence and read aloud.

Not too long after page eleven, the Reeds sent Jane Eyre away to Lowood, a school for poor, parentless girls with willful dispositions.

"Willful disposition!" Jemmie fumed. "Those Reeds were just mean to her, is all."

And did Jane like Lowood? How could she? "'The scanty supply of food was distressing,'" I read. "'We never stirred beyond the garden walls except to go to church.'" What Jane was saying in her fancy, polite way was that Lowood was cold and boring and that there was nothing to eat there but bread and burnt oatmeal.

"Maybe they don't feed 'em right on account of their bad dispositions," Jemmie said.

"I don't know. My mother cooks over at the children's shelter. Lou Anne goes along sometimes and does the girls' hair. She says some of the older runaways could kill you, they look at you so mean. But they all get fed plenty."

We got so wrapped up in the book that we forgot all about Lou Anne and Nana Grace and getting caught. We were starting chapter six when it happened. Jane was still freezing and starving at Lowood. "'The next day commenced as before,'" Jemmie began from her side of the fence, "'getting up and dressing by rushlight; but this morning we were obliged to dispense with the ceremony of washing: the water in the pitchers was frozen.'"

Nana Grace's voice cut in. "I just couldn't drowse off." I heard her walk down the steps. Suddenly it went quiet on the other side of the fence. Then Nana Grace said, "What'd you just slide under your butt, child?"

"Nothing, Nana. A book."

"There somethin' wrong with it? Give it here." I peeked through the knothole. Nana Grace was riffling the pages with her lips pursed. "Sure got a lot of fancy words in it. Where's it from?"

"A friend."

"From over the old place?"

"No, ma'am."

Nana Grace closed *Jane Eyre*. "Where'd you get this book?"

"From a friend here. Her name is Cass." Jemmie practically put her finger in my eye. "If you look through this knothole you can meet her."

Nana Grace squared her shoulders. "You bring her on around. I don't meet folks by peepin' through holes."

"Come on, Cass," Jemmie called.

I prayed that Lou Anne wasn't watching, and I slipped around the fence.

"Nana," Jemmie said, "this is our neighbor, Cass Bodine."

Because of her bossy voice I had thought of Nana Grace as kind of big, but standing beside her, I realized that she was no taller than me. She looked me up and down, then stuck out her hand. "I'm pleased to meet you, Cass Bodine." Her hand was as cool and dry as the pages of *Jane Eyre*.

"I'm pleased to meet you too, Miss Grace."

"Oh, call me Nana," she said. "Everybody else does."

Jemmie was shifting from one foot to the other. "You won't tell Mom about Cass, will you, Nana?"

Nana Grace squinted one eye at Jemmie. "An' why not?"

Jemmie made lines in the dust with her bare toes. "You know how she feels about the fence, the way she calls Cass's family a bunch of redneck bigots."

When she said that I felt like I'd had the wind knocked out of me.

"Jemmeal!" Nana scolded.

"You know she does!"

Nana Grace stared at Jemmie until Jemmie looked away, and then Nana Grace turned to me. Her brown eyes were pale and flecked with green. "I hope you'll understand. When Jemmie's mama was growing up, Tallahassee was a whole 'nother place. Seemed like black and white folks had a war going. Jemmie's mama was just little then, but she got caught in the crossfire. She ain't learned to forgive yet."

"But you did, didn't you, Nana?" Jemmie hugged her grandmother around the waist.

"You get as old as me," she said, stroking Jemmie's arm, "forgive is the only thing you can do. Black, white, red, yellow, or sky-blue-pink, we are all God's children." She took my hand again and gave it a squeeze. "Child, you feel free to come over anytime."

Lou Anne caught us the next day. She'd stepped outside to see if her friend, Carey, was walking up the road yet, and she heard Jemmie reading to me from the other side of the fence. She walked across the yard. "Who is that talking to you?" She leaned past me, peeked through the knothole, then fell back. "My goodness." She bit her lip and looked again. "Daddy know about this?" she whispered.

When I said no, she headed back to the house, shaking her head. I followed her.

"Please don't tell him, Lou Anne. You know how he is." We kept whispering, as if Daddy could hear us all the way from his job at the Live Oak Apartments.

She opened the front door. "But if I don't tell, it'd be like lying."

"Not if he doesn't ask."

We went inside and sat down on the sofa. Lou Anne twisted a strand of hair around her finger. "That girl over there, is she nice?"

"Real nice. You'd like her."

A car pulled up out front. The horn blew. Lou Anne and I ran to the front door. It was Carey.

"Hey, Lou!" Carey yelled. Her wavy brown hair brushed the car door as she leaned out the window. "I got my brother's car. We can go to Movies Eight for a matinee if you think Missy'll keep quiet."

"I'll watch Missy," I said quickly. "You two go on."

Lou Anne's face lit up. "Thanks, Cass." Then she frowned. "But that doesn't mean I won't tell. I have to think about it."

But Lou Anne didn't tell, and after that I started going over to Jemmie's house for a while each day.

I had been in Miss Liz's house plenty of times. When I was little, Miss Liz would invite me to tea parties in her best parlor—Ben, too, until my father told him boys don't go to tea parties.

I would sit at one end of her long rosewood table, Miss Liz at the other. On the in-between chairs were her porcelain dolls. We had to put pillows under them so they could see over the table edge. Each one had her own little cup and plate. "Would you care to pour the tea, Miss Catherine?" Miss Liz would say, and I would pour a little into each cup. The dolls didn't eat or drink much, but they all smiled like they were happy to be there.

Miss Liz had made all the dolls herself, except for Hattie, who she had had since she was little. She let me help her make dolls sometimes. Miss Liz had a special upstairs room where she made her dolls. The dolly room. That was Jemmie's room now.

The first thing Jemmie did when I started visiting her was drag me to her closet. "You gotta see this." Miss Liz's family had taken all the whole dolls off the shelves, but they had left lots of parts behind. "Need a leg?" She opened a box. "I got about thirty of 'em. Arms too."

I picked up a small box. "Here's eyeballs." I showed her the way the glass eyes were weighted so they'd open and close.

Jemmie blinked and the glass eyes blinked back. "Creepy," she said. She climbed up on a chair so she could reach things on the top shelf. "Cass, look at this!" She handed me a black doll with a kerchief tied around her head and an apron over a blue-and-white checked dress. "Why would Miss Liz have a black doll?"

Holding the doll, I felt like I was looking at an old friend. "This is Hattie," I said. I put my nose up to her checked dress and breathed in. She still smelled like Miss Liz's lilac perfume.

"Hattie?" Jemmie climbed off the chair and took the doll back. "She looks like she was played with a whole lot."

"She was Miss Liz's favorite doll. There used to be a real Hattie who took care of Miss Liz and her sister, Cora, when they were little. Miss Liz said she cried more when Hattie died than she did when her own mama passed."

Jemmie flopped down on the bed. "Hattie was still a servant." She laid the doll down so her head was on the bed pillow—just like she used to lie on Miss Liz's bed. "From now on she's not Hattie, she's Queen Moustafa of Africa."

As Queen Moustafa, Hattie looked different. Her black painted eyes were suddenly fierce and proud.

When Nana Grace came in with a laundry basket on her hip, Jemmie introduced her to the new queen.

"Don't she look nice," Nana Grace said, smoothing Hattie's skirt and apron with one hand. "Now, would you two like to help an old lady paint her bedroom?"

We left Queen Moustafa staring at the ceiling and followed Nana Grace up a narrow flight of stairs. She had chosen the tiny room at the top of the house for her bedroom. No one had used that room at all since the original Hattie.

"What a pretty color," I said, dipping my brush in a bucket of blue paint.

"It's called Blue Skies," Nana Grace said. "I'm practicing for heaven."

"What color is your room?" Jemmie asked me, like it was some faraway place she would never see.

"Puke pink. Lou Anne's choice."

Jemmie and me used brushes to paint the edges of the walls and the corners. As Nana Grace ran a roller over the walls, she sang, "Oh wasn't that a wide river...that river of Jordan. Wasn't that a mighty wide river...one more river to cross."

I asked her about the river of Jordan in the song.

"Crossing Jordan used to be a secret code for freedom," she said. "Slaves couldn't talk about their freedom right out so they hid talk of it here and there." As she ran the roller across the wall it spit flecks of paint so Nana Grace had tiny blue freckles all over her dark arms. "Freedom dreams," she said, running the roller in long strokes. "They was always hid in plain sight for anyone who knew how to look and how to listen."

It took us a couple of hours to finish the job. We set down our brushes. "Now, ain't that pretty," Nana Grace said. Even the ceiling was heavenly blue.

"Over at the mall you can get stick-on stars that glow in the dark," I said.

Nana Grace crossed her arms like she was giving herself a hug. "I'd like that just fine," she said, gazing up at her new blue ceiling.

When Miss Liz's folks had picked through the house, they hadn't touched a thing in Hattie's room. The straight-back chair and trunk and even Hattie's bed were all still there. When there was no more danger that we'd drip paint on it, Nana Grace carried in her own prize quilt from the hall. "This was made by my grandmother." She shook it out, and the bright quilt drifted down, dressing up Hattie's old bed. "Nana Ivy was a seamstress. Made all kind of fancy clothes for rich white folks. This quilt got little bits of ball dresses and wedding gowns in it, lawn-party dresses, and go-to-the-show getups." She stroked the slinky satins and mossy velvets like she was patting a cat.

"How about these?" I asked, pointing. Scattered among the fancy fabrics were scraps that were plain and worn.

"Family patches," she said.

Each family patch had something embroidered on it. Sometimes just a name, like Nesta Louise, or Uncle Henry Clay, but sometimes there were a few words along with the name. There was a pink patch that said Baby Dora Gone To Jesus, and a blue one sprigged with red flowers that said Melba Owen married July 8, 1902. One scrap of gray flannel said Martin Clay a free man.

I fingered that patch. "What's this one mean?" I asked.

Nana Grace sat down in Hattie's chair and spread the edge of the quilt over her knees. "Martin Clay was born a slave, died a free man. Got a whole lotta history and a whole lotta family stitched into this quilt. What we forget, the quilt remembers."

～

From Nana Grace's window you could look down into my yard like the fence wasn't even there. Sometimes, like on the weekends when we couldn't see each other, Jemmie said she would look out that window to see what I was up to. She didn't always see me. Sometimes she saw other Bodines. "That sister of yours has the prettiest hair in the world," she'd say the next time she saw me, or, "Your daddy's bald spot looks like a flashlight when the sun hits it right."

The morning after Andy Thompson had picked up Lou Anne for a date in his daddy's Malibu she said, "That boy is uh-gly. If your sister doesn't look out, he's gonna give her warts."

I rolled my eyes. "Lou Anne thinks he's a dream."

Jemmie snorted. "Nightmare, maybe. He's skinny and his teeth stick out. And his driving is just plain sorry."

"He drives okay."

"Good as any other white guy."

"Meaning what?"

"They drive like this, white guys do." She sat up stiff in Hattie's old straight-back chair with her arms out, elbows locked.

"What's wrong with that?"

"It looks dumb, is all. Andy doesn't do a thing but sit there like an old stick."

"How do black guys drive?"

"They drive cool." She slid down on her tailbone and hung one wrist over the imaginary wheel. "They look under the steering wheel. They crank the radio, they roll the window down, and they hang an elbow out. 'Hey, baby,' they say, 'you're lookin' mighty fine. How's your bad, black self?'"

I giggled. "Do you know what Andy says?"

"Last night I heard him yell, 'Lou Anne? I have the car until seven. Want to go to the Dairy Queen?'" Jemmie shook her head. "Pitiful. That's the only word that describes it." As she stood and stretched, her tank top rode up to her ribs. "Want to go to my mother's room and do something on the computer?"

"Your mother has her own computer?" I asked, following her down the hall. I'd never seen one outside of the school computer lab and the public library.

"It belongs to my mother and me. I wanted a trampoline, but she said to get a decent education you got to have a computer."

"Does Nana Grace use it?"

"Nana says it's the devil's tool. She doesn't touch it." We walked into her mother's bedroom.

"This was Miss Liz's room," I told Jemmie. "She slept in it for eighty years, ever since her parents died and her sister married one of the Jenkins boys." But there was nothing of Miss Liz's left in the room. The walls, which had always been a violety gray Miss Liz called Wisteria, were now plain old white. The blue cologne bottles Miss Liz used to let me open and sniff, her little statue of the Eiffel Tower, and the postcard collection she gathered on her world tour in 1939 were all gone. There was no clutter at all. Except for a couple of shelves of books and some pictures by the bed, it was as clean and empty as a hospital room.

I looked at the pictures. One showed Jemmie and her mother and a man I bet was her father. He was thin and really tall. He looked like the runners from Kenya—the fastest in the world, according to my running magazine. He had a funny mark on one side of his face. I hoped she would tell me about him.

She purposely pointed at a different picture. "That's my mother at her college graduation." The young woman in the photo wore a navy blue gown and a mortarboard on her head. Every spring there are flocks of students dressed like that all over Tallahassee.

"Is that you?" I pointed to another one.

"No, that's my mother when she was about five years old." The little girl was sitting on a woman's lap. The woman had shiny black hair smoothed back and twisted into a bun. She wore a white uniform. Jemmie said, "That's Nana Grace."

"Nana was pretty. Was she a nurse, too?"

"Nuh-uh. Nana ran the hospital laundry. See?" She handed me a picture of a little girl sitting on a huge stack of folded sheets. "That's my mother at Nana's laundry. She used to go along. She'd play in the laundry room and out in the alley behind where the dryers blew out. The lint would drift up just like snow. One time the little girl of one of the nurses came out back, too. They made feather beds for their dolls with the lint. Nana even fed the girl lunch, but when the girl brought my mother inside the hospital, the nurse forbid her to play with my mother. 'Black children are stupid and dirty,' she said, 'they have germs.' My mother cried. She told Nana she was going to take an ax and chop the hospital into little pieces."

"How could anyone be that mean to a little girl?" I asked. "I'll bet Nana Grace told that nurse off good."

"She says you didn't talk back in those days, not if you wanted to keep your job. But she talked to my mother and told her that if she worked hard, she could become a nurse herself. That would show the world who was stupid." Jemmie walked over to the computer and pushed the button. "Nana believes in education, even though she only got to the seventh grade herself. She says I'm gonna be a doctor."

"A doctor?" I looked at Jemmie with a whole new respect.

"That's what Nana says. What do your parents want you to be?"

When my mother talked about work, she said the main thing was to work hard and be honest. My father said you should work for yourself if you don't want to take crap from a bunch of people who don't know what they're talking about. I couldn't remember them ever saying Lou Anne or me were going to be anything special. "Lou Anne wants to be a beautician."

The computer hummed. "Yeah? You want to be one too?" Jemmie asked.

"No way."

"Well, what do you want to be?"

"I like science," I said. "Maybe I could be a scientist."

"You've got to go to college, then."

There are three colleges in Tallahassee, and students are all over the place. Some of them rent houses in our neighborhood. It's all college students in the apartment complex where Daddy works, but I never imagined myself growing up to be one of them. When the computer finished booting up, the screen was bluer than Nana Grace's heavenly blue room. "I don't know," I said, staring at the screen. "No one in my family's ever been to college."

Jemmie looked surprised. "Not even junior college?"

"No."

Nana Grace carried in a vase of pink roses she'd cut off Miss Liz's Queen Elizabeth rosebush.

"Cass says nobody in her family's ever been to college," Jemmie told her.

"Nothin' strange about that. Your mother was the first in ours," Nana said, arranging the flowers. "Maybe Cass is gonna be the first in hers."

I shook my head no. "Costs too much."

"Not as much as ignorance, child. You pay for an education one time. You pay for ignorance your whole life long." Before leaving the room, she put her hand on my shoulder. "Smart girl like you could be anything you want."

"You could get a scholarship," Jemmie said. "An athletic scholarship for running."

"You too. We'll be the fastest runners to ever hit college."

Jemmie punched my arm and winked. "Chocolate Milk," she said. "Let's check E-mail." She moved the mouse like lightning, clicking on things. "Hey, Terrence wrote."

"Who's Terrence?"

"He's my British pen pal. My mother won't let me go into chat rooms or anything like that, but she found a site that hooks kids up with each other all over the world."

We read the note from Terrence. He bragged about a darts tournament he had been in and how he had hit twenty-seven bull's-eyes in a row. "Terry thinks that tossing darts is a sport," Jemmie said. "Why don't we write him back about our running?" We took turns typing sentences. She told him how we ran for miles and miles in hundred-degree heat.

"We never ran miles and miles," I said.

"An' Terry probably never hit twenty-seven bull's-eyes either," she answered, typing another line about how good we were.

After that we wrote pretty much anything that came into our heads. Jemmie even included the fact that we were going to get running scholarships to college, which made me a little breathless. In my house we talked about college like it was only for other people who had more money or better luck, not for us. But reading what Jemmie wrote, I thought that maybe I could go.

~

When I got home Lou Anne was feeding the baby.

"What's it like over there?" she asked, sticking a spoonful of strained pears in Missy's mouth.

"Well, they're painting the inside of the house and fixing it all up."

Most of the pears came right back out. "Missy!" Lou Anne scraped the pears off the baby's chin and tried again. "You know what I mean, Cass. Is it different or anything?"

"You mean because they're black?" I shaped a hamburger patty and set it on a plate. "Why don't you come over and see for yourself?."

"And have Daddy ground me for the rest of my life? No, thank you."

CHAPTER SEVEN

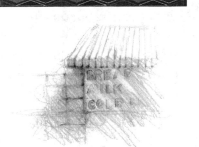

What's in Her Pockets?

Jemmie and me were on the steps. Nana Grace sat on the porch above us rocking slowly back and forth and fanning herself and the baby in her arms with a section of the newspaper. "S'posed to hit ninety-six today."

"Feels like a hundred and ninety-six," Jemmie said, tugging my hair hard.

"Ow!"

"Wouldya hold still, Cass?" Jemmie was trying to braid my hair into lots of little braids like hers. "That doesn't look right," she said. "Your hair's too slippery." She took the braids out for the umpteenth time and started over. My scalp was beginning to tingle.

"Ninety-six degrees," Nana repeated. "Tallahassee's gotta be the hottest place on God's green earth. You ever seen snow, Cass?"

"Only in the movies," I gasped. Jemmie was making my eyes water, she was pulling so hard.

"That don't count. You gotta smell snow, you gotta feel it on yer skin," Nana said. "I only seen it once myself. I was visiting my husband's people in Philadelphia. I ran out and stood on the sidewalk catching snowflakes on my tongue."

"What did they taste like?" I asked.

"Sharp," she said. "Kinda like sucking on a penny."

Talking about that trip reminded her of a recipe she had gotten from one of her husband's aunts while she was up there. "She called it Brownstone Cake and it was the best chocolate cake I ever tasted. You put vanilla ice cream between the layers," she said. "I could do with a piece of that right about now. How'd you two like to help me whip one up?"

"Sure," I said. I would have volunteered to jump off the roof to get Jemmie to quit pulling my hair.

Nana held out two wrinkled dollars. "If we're gonna make a Brownstone Cake somebody gotta fetch the eggs for it. Any volunteers?"

"We'll go, Nana. Cass's hair is hopeless." Jemmie stuffed the money in the pocket of her shorts. She unbraided the strands she had been working on and we started out for the USA store.

"Mr. G. is the manager," I said as we walked along. "He's Indian."

"His name's Mr. Gee?"

"He told us to call him that, since no one can pronounce his name right. He's nice."

We walked slowly, trying to stick to the shady spots. At a hundred and ninety-six degrees, it was too hot to run.

As we walked across the tar parking lot of the convenience store, heat bounced off it in waves.

"Look, Jemmie." I pointed out one of the advertisements that was plastered to the store windows. "The lottery's up to fourteen million."

"We never buy tickets. My mother says playing the lottery is like throwing your money away."

"Is not." I peered through the window trying to see Mr. G.'s shiny black hair. "One time we won sixty dollars." Instead of Mr. G.'s black hair, I saw Andy Thompson's carrot top. "Oh, shoot. Andy's behind the counter. I'll stay out here so he doesn't see the two of us together and get us in trouble."

I sat on the curb and waited while Jemmie went inside. A mockingbird scolded me from its perch on the telephone wire. It flew away when a car drove by dragging its muffler. A lady in a pair of pink bedroom slippers scuffed across the parking lot and dropped some coins in the pay phone. "Germaine?" she said in a drippy-sweet voice, "Germaine, honey? This is Latoya." She talked and she talked. She smoked and crushed out two cigarettes with the toe of her slipper before she hung up and scuffed away.

Jemmie was taking an awfully long time to get those eggs. I went and peeked around the lottery poster to see what was keeping her. She was up at the counter all right, but Andy had one hand on either side of her carton of eggs like he was guarding it. As he talked, he was getting redder and redder, especially his ears. His face was so close to hers, he had to be spraying her with spit.

I pushed the door open and the bell tinkled. Andy and Jemmie both looked my way. "Hi, Andy," I said.

"Be with ya in a minute, Cass, right after I deal with this little problem." He turned back to Jemmie. "I know what I saw, and I saw you pocket something."

I felt cold all over. Daddy always said for black people, stealing's as easy as breathing.

"Did not," she said. The glare she gave him must have scorched his eyelashes. "Get your eyes checked."

I took a deep breath. She didn't do it. I knew she didn't. Jemmie was different than Daddy said.

"Then you won't mind if I check your pockets," Andy said, and I thought how dumb he was going to look with his hands inside her empty pockets.

But Jemmie stuck her chin out. "You can just keep your cruddy hands out of my pockets."

Andy crossed his arms and leaned back. "I thought so."

Maybe she did do it, I thought then. Maybe it was just like Daddy said. Maybe Jemmie was no different.

Andy looked at Jemmie like he would look at the sole of his shoe after he'd stepped in something. "We have two choices here. The easy way is I check your pockets. The hard way is I call the police." He put a hand on the phone. "Which'll it be?"

Police! They would roar up with their sirens blaring and take Jemmie away.

Even though my knees were shaking, I walked over and stood beside her. "Andy," I said, "this is my friend." Seemed like everything from the quarts of oil to the bags of potato chips sat up and took notice when I said the word "friend."

Andy sure noticed. "Your friend?"

I put my arm around her shoulders. "Her name is Jemmie Lewis. She goes to my school and we run together. She's the fastest."

He snickered. "Not fast enough. I caught her putting something in her pocket. Your friend here has sticky fingers."

"She does not," I said, and I plunged a hand into each of her pockets. I felt clear down to the seams. "She doesn't have a thing that belongs to you. Just money for the eggs." I turned her pockets inside out to show him that he was wrong, but as I did it I felt ashamed. I wasn't any better than Andy. I knew Jemmie, and still I hadn't been sure. That only made me madder at Andy.

"You apologize to her," I demanded, slapping the dollars down on the counter.

"For what? I was just doing my job. She shoulda showed me there was nothing in her pockets."

He rang up the eggs and made change—which he gave to me. "You know how it is, Cass. These kids come in here, they snitch some gum, a pack of baseball cards. Small stuff, but it adds up."

"And you never have a white kid do that?" Jemmie asked.

"You have a nice day now, Cass." Andy put the eggs in a bag. "Say hey to Lou Anne for me."

I took the eggs and grabbed Jemmie by the arm. "Come on, let's get out of here." We marched out, but my knees were still shaking.

Outside, Jemmie kicked a rock. "Antipathy is way too good for him." The pebble sailed across the parking lot and skipped all the way to the stripe in the middle of the road. "That Andy needs to be eviscerated."

"What's ee-viscerated?" It wasn't a *Jane Eyre* word.

"Eviscerated is when you yank somebody's guts out." Jemmie jerked her leg back and kicked another rock. "Like through their nose or their ears."

"Gross. You're going to make me barf." All I wanted to do was sit down on the curb and hug my knees. "How do you do it?" I asked. "How do you stay so cool? You weren't even scared when Andy said he was going to call the police."

Jemmie nudged another pebble with the toe of her sneaker. "I was scared."

"You didn't look it. You looked like you were going to eviscerate him all over Mr. G.'s nice, clean counter."

"I could've cried, but I didn't let myself. Not in front of that jerk, Andy."

"You were gonna cry?"

"You think you're the only one who gets scared?" she asked, then punched my arm. "You tell anyone about that, though, and I'll eviscerate you. Come on," she said. "Let's traverse." She turned and ran down the sidewalk, the soles of her sneakers flashing. I carefully tucked the bag under my arm and chased after her.

All the way home I felt bad. If the same thing had happened with Ben, I would've known he didn't do it. I hadn't trusted Jemmie, not all the way. I ran fast, but the bad feeling kept up. I couldn't outrun it.

⁓

Even though we were all sweaty, we were still running when we got back to the house. Nana Grace was on the porch dozing with Artie on her lap. She opened her eyes. "You two look all down in the mouth. Somethin' wrong?"

Jemmie told her about Andy, about how she'd stood in front of him with her pockets hanging out, and about how I'd stuck up for her.

At first, Nana Grace didn't say a thing, just shook her head. "Come on inside," she said at last. She put the baby into his high chair and sprinkled a few Cheerios on the tray to keep him busy, then she cracked three of the eggs we'd brought her into a bowl. As she whipped them with a fork she stared off as if she was seeing something from a long time ago. She set the fork down and reached across and took Jemmie's hand. "Child, you done good standin' up like that." Then she grabbed my hand with her other one and gave it a squeeze. "You too, Cass. I'm proud of the both of you."

Jemmie sat on a stool swinging her legs, kicking the rail with her heels. "Only thing I did was try to buy eggs. Andy went and made a federal case out of it. It ain't right."

"No, it ain't." Nana Grace poured flour and sugar and milk into the bowl and passed it to me. "Three hundred strokes, child." She put her empty hands in her lap and her shoulders sagged. "Used to be worse, though. Used to be you went in a white store, they didn't have to sell you a thing 'less they felt like it. Back then we had separate bathrooms, separate water fountains, separate everything. We rode at the back of the bus then. And we didn't sit at all if there was a white person needed a seat."

Then she told us about Rosa Parks. I knew about her from school, about how one day in Montgomery, Alabama, she refused to give her seat up to a white man, but it sounded more real when Nana Grace told it. "Miss Rosa wasn't tryin' to cause a fuss," Nana said. "She was just tired. Tired from work, and tired of the way things was, I guess. Seemed like no big thing, one black woman on one bus wouldn't give up her seat. But what Rosa Parks did was like holdin' a match to tinder. Seemed for a time like the whole South might go up."

Jemmie put her elbows on her knees, her chin in her hands. "Was there trouble here too?"

"Sure was." She glanced my way. "Get your finger out of my batter, Cass."

"Sorry, Nana." I sucked my finger clean. "What happened here?"

"Same kinda thing. Here it was a coupla black college girls took seats at the front of the bus. In them days there was a line on the bus floor. Black folks was supposed to stay back of that line, even if the back of the bus was full. Oh, there was some spillin' over sometimes, 'specially on the routes that went to the black neighborhoods. But the thing you never could do was take a seat alongside a white rider, and that's just what them girls did, sat down in the same seat as a white woman. Driver told 'em to go stand in back with the rest."

"Did they go?" Jemmie asked.

"No, ma'am. They said they paid their ten cents same as everybody else and they meant to sit. The bus driver had 'em arrested."

I stopped stirring. "They got arrested for sitting?"

"Police said they was tryin' to cause a riot. Word went out, stay off the bus. Just like that, we was on strike. Well, stayin' off of the bus was hard. We still had to get to work some kinda way. But like the Reverend Steele said, 'We'd rather walk in dignity than ride in humiliation.'"

"So you walked to work?" I asked.

"A lotta folks used their feet, but I had too far to go so I shared a ride. I got poked by elbows and knees, there was so many of us shoved in. We did what we had to do to get to work and we stayed off the bus."

"Why'd they care so much about a little thing like where we sat on the bus?" Jemmie asked.

"Because if we sat where we wanted on the bus, then we might do the same at lunch counters and in movie theaters. We might forget to drink out of the water fountain that said Colored over it. We might think we was equal."

I stared into the bowl. I felt like I was somehow part of the bad things that had happened because I was white. Nana Grace put a hand on my shoulder. "Now, Cass," she said, "I remember three white boys who got arrested for sitting beside blacks on the bus. Two of them did jail time. And there wasn't a whole lot of black lawyers back then, so we got most of our legal help from white lawyers. Most worked for free, too."

"And you won, didn't you?" I said.

"Inch by inch. It was like tryin' to take a bone away from a dog." She popped the lid off a can of shortening and tore a corner off a paper towel with an angry jerk. "Grease the pans, would you, child?" She shoved the shortening and the scrap of towel at Jemmie.

Slowly, the wrinkles between her eyebrows evened out. "It drug on and on, but we endured. The city and the state of Florida threw every crazy thing in our path they could think of, but the Supreme Court was on our side. It was just a matter of time."

"Did anyone get hurt?" Jemmie asked.

"Oh, it got ugly sometimes. Windows got broke. Crosses got burned in folks' yards. Mamas had to take their children to the middle of the house, afraid what might happen if they got near a window."

She folded her hands in front of her on the table. "I remember the first time I rode the bus after the strike like it was yesterday. I thought my heart would bust, I was so scared, but I sat right down on the long bench seat, smack behind the driver. When he looked in his mirror, he saw my black face lookin' right back at him. I could tell he wasn't happy. Wasn't nothin' he could do about it, though. I was up front and I meant to stay there. It had been a mighty long walk from the back of the bus."

Jemmie set the greased pans on the table. "I guess things have gotten better."

"Yes, they have. A whole lot better. We gained a lot of ground over the years, but what ain't happened yet is blacks and whites gettin' easy with each other." She poured the batter into the pans. "White and black are like oil and water. You can stir us together, but we don't stay mixed."

I could see the rumpled backs of her stockings as she bent down to slide the pans into the oven. "To tell the truth, I about gave up on it," she said, "then along comes you two." She stood up and looked from me to Jemmie. "Seein' the way you get along has me thinkin' one day it's gonna be different; one day it's gonna be just fine."

My smile felt pasted on. If Nana Grace could see into my heart, she would know that when Andy accused Jemmie of stealing I hadn't really trusted her. I had had to check her pockets to be sure.

CHAPTER EIGHT

It is a Great Pleasure to See You

Nana Grace sent us back to the USA store the very next morning. "Hold your head up," she told Jemmie. "You got a right to be there, same as anybody else."

"Nana...it's a hundred and forty-seven degrees out," Jemmie whined.

"Doin' the right thing ain't always comfortable." She held the door for us. "Now you scoot on down there and bring back a loaf of bread, no excuses." So off we went with Nana watching us.

As soon as we were out of her sight we slowed down. We weren't in a hurry to get there.

Before going inside, we snuck a look around the posters. "No Andy," I said. "That's Mr. G. dusting the cigarette rack with a feather duster. He has a kind of fancy foreign way of talking."

"I don't care if he speaks pig Latin," Jemmie said, "as long as he's not Andy." She opened the door.

Mr. G. had set down his duster to wait on a fat lady with a striped plastic purse. "It is glorious weather, is it not?" he asked, putting her roach spray in a bag and folding the top over neatly.

Jemmie got her bread and we stepped up to the counter. "Miss Catherine Bodine," he said, flashing his square white teeth at me in a dazzling smile. "It is a very great pleasure to see you."

"Good to see you too, Mr. G. This is my friend, Jemmie."

Mr. G. flashed his toothy smile at Jemmie too. "I am enormously pleased to make your acquaintance, Miss Jemmie." He touched his fingertips together like he was going to pray and made a stiff little bow from the waist. "Are you perhaps a runner like Miss Catherine?"

"Yes, sir. We run together. We're a team. Chocolate Milk."

"Chocolate Milk?" He looked confused. "To me it is a drink—which I sell in pints and quarts—not two lovely young ladies."

Jemmie put her brown arm next to my white one.

"Ah!" Mr. G. snapped his fingers. "I understand now. Chocolate Milk. Clever indeed."

Jemmie paid him for the bread. Mr. G. put the loaf in a bag and folded the top just like he had for the lady. He handed each of us a mint. "It has been a very great pleasure to meet you, Miss Jemmie. Now that you know the way, do not be a stranger." And he bowed again.

Jemmie bowed back. We left the USA store sucking our mints.

"See, that wasn't so bad," I said.

"No," said Jemmie, "Mr. G. is okay, once you get used to the way he talks."

"It's Andy who's a jerk," I said.

"A super jerk." Jemmie swung the bread bag back and forth like she meant to sling it up over the telephone wires. "What does Lou Anne like about him, anyway?"

"She thinks he's cute."

Jemmie gagged.

When we came to the vacant lot where I always picked flowers for Miss Liz I could see some nice black-eyed Susans and daisies in the high grass. "You wanna meet Miss Liz?" I asked.

Jemmie looked at me like I was crazy. "It's a little late for that, isn't it?"

"No, it's not." We picked the flowers, then cut across the parking lot of the Presbyterian church and into the graveyard. Her white stone was speckled with sunlight. "Hi, Miss Liz." It was nice and cool under the oaks. I put the flowers in the pickle jar. "Miss Liz, this is Jemmie Lewis, the girl who lives in your house. Jemmie, this is Miss Liz."

"Elizabeth Latitia Faircloth," Jemmie read off the stone. "I'm pleased to meet you." Then she told me to come sit on the sofa.

What she was calling the sofa was Miss Liz's nearest neighbor, Henry Hudson DeWitt. Henry Hudson wasn't buried in the ground like most everyone else, including Miss Liz. He had a marble box that sat on top of the ground. Jemmie had boosted herself up and was sitting cross-legged on top of it. "Come on," she said, slapping the stone beside her. "Park it."

"Don't you think that's kind of disrespectful?"

"No, we're visiting. We'll visit H. H. too."

"Well, okay." The stone was cool on my bare legs. I turned so I could read the writing on the marble lid. "Henry Hudson DeWitt: Father, soldier, railroad man. Called Home. What do you think he died of?"

Jemmie stuck her tongue in her cheek and thought. "Fell off of a train?"

"Jemmie! You shouldn't make jokes about dead people."

"Okay, okay. Heart attack, maybe?" She clutched her chest, rolled her eyes up, and flopped back across the top of Henry Hudson DeWitt's box.

"Jemmie Lewis!"

She sat back up. "Doesn't look like folks visit him much." There wasn't one single flower. Not even a plastic one anywhere near his marble box.

"Maybe all his people died too."

We walked around the graveyard. We found plenty of Montgomerys, and lots of Faircloths, all shoulder-to-shoulder around Miss Liz. There were twenty-six Masons, without even counting the row of baby graves with lambs on them. But there were no more DeWitts. Just H. H. all by himself.

Jemmie took a couple of flowers out of Miss Liz's jar. She laid them on Henry Hudson's coffin with the stems crossed right about where she figured his chest was. "There," she said. "Now it's okay to sit on his box while we chat with Miss Liz."

I don't know whether spirits stay right by their own graves, but talking to her stone was easier than talking to the air. "Jemmie sleeps in the dolly room," I told the marble stone.

"That's right," said Jemmie, talking to the stone, too. "Your relatives took all the dolls, except for Hattie. Hope you don't mind, I renamed her

Queen Moustafa. Hattie's okay, but it's a servant name. It's time she found her true self."

"Huh," I said, closing my eyes and making my voice sound all creaky, "Hattie was always good enough for her when I knew her. No need to give her airs."

Jemmie blinked. "You getting weird on me, Cass? Don't tell me Miss Liz is talking through you. It'd be too spooky."

"Nah, I just know her, is all, and I don't think she would want you changing Hattie's name around." Then I said, "Darned right I wouldn't," in my scratchy Miss Liz voice. "But if my good-for-nothing relatives left my doll supplies, you can make yourself an African queen. I have all the parts you need." Surprised, I shut my mouth. Now where did that come from? Didn't seem like I'd thought it up.

"Thank you, ma'am, I'll just do that." Jemmie jumped down from the stone. "See you later, Miss Liz. You too, H. H. Don't you two go anywhere."

All the way home Jemmie talked about the African queen doll she was going to make for herself.

"I don't really think there are parts in there to make an African queen doll," I said.

"So I'll use a Magic Marker if I have to. But I bet I'll find the parts I need. Miss Liz said so."

Trouble

Miss Liz hadn't lied. There were enough parts in the closet to make a black doll. Just one. Not a baby or a woman, but a doll of a girl about our age. There were plenty of parts for white dolls. I decided to make a doll the same age as Jemmie's so our dolls could be friends too. We sat cross-legged on Jemmie's bed, working on our dolls and reading *Jane Eyre*.

Jane was out of the orphanage now. She was eighteen years old and working as a governess for a Mr. Rochester. The girl she was governess for wasn't Mr. Rochester's actual daughter, she was his ward, which meant he was just raising her. "I think Jane's getting a crush on Mr. Rochester," Jemmie said after a while.

"No way!" I was stuffing my doll's body with sawdust, trying not to spill any on Jemmie's bedspread, but I set it down and took the book off Jemmie's lap and flipped back a few pages. "Here it is, the part about his face. It says right here he has broad and jetty brows, and big nostrils. It says his face is grim and square. Even Jane says he doesn't have a very pleasing phys-i-og-no-my. She's talking about the way he looked. If she wasn't so polite, she'd just come out and say it. Mr. Rochester is butt-ugly."

"So what?" Jemmie leaned back on her arms. "She could like him anyway. Being good-looking isn't the only thing that's important. My father had a scar all the way from his scalp to his mouth, so I guess you could say he was ugly. But it didn't matter to us. We thought he looked just fine."

I remembered the photo in her mother's room. So that *was* her father. I had purposely never asked Jemmie about him. After all, I wouldn't want her asking me if my daddy had run off. But since she had brought him up, I blurted out, "Where is your father, anyway?"

"Dead." She started shoving sawdust into the cotton body of her doll so hard I thought she'd bust the seams. "He died last year, right before Christmas. Cancer got him. He always wanted us to have someplace of our own, so my mother took the insurance money and put it down on this house."

I didn't know what to say. I never thought that her father might be dead. "How'd he get the scar?"

"It happened when he was in high school. He was walking home one night, late. He got surrounded by a group of white boys. At first they just called him names. Then they started to shove him around. If he could've broke through, he could've outrun every one of them, but they blocked him with their arms. Then one of the guys pulled a knife."

I picked at the tufts on Jemmie's bedspread, trying to imagine what it would be like to be treated that way just because of the color of my skin. "Seems like being black has been the whole history of your family, Jemmie."

"My dad used to say that being black was like carrying something heavy all the time, something you couldn't set down. If you're black, he said, you could work hard, but at the end of the day all you got was tired."

I sprawled belly-down on the bed and rested my chin on the backs of hands. "It's like that for us, too. My folks work all the time, but we don't ever get ahead."

"It is *not* the same."

Jemmie sounded mad, but I didn't know why.

"Y'all could get ahead if you wanted to," she said. "You're white. You don't have a thing in the world stopping you."

I felt as if she had slapped me. "Plenty of things stop people, not just the color of their skin. Not having money can stop you cold."

"People don't disrespect you just because you don't have money."

"Do too! Most of the college kids who live in the apartments where my daddy works couldn't fix a leaky faucet if they had to, but they treat him like dirt, and you know what? He can't say one thing. He needs the job." My voice was getting high and shaky, but I went right on. "And my mother? She buys everything with coupons. One time I saw her cry over the electric bill." I heard what I was saying and I was ashamed. Daddy would say I was doing the family wash in public. The worst part of it was, it didn't make a bit of difference to Jemmie.

"It's not the same," she said, and she stood up and walked over to the window. "You don't understand."

I could just see her profile, and for a moment I saw what my father would see, someone completely different from me. Someone I didn't know at all. "I got to go," I stumbled to my feet, but as I turned toward the door I heard the squeal of brakes.

"Oh no, Cass. It's your dad." Jemmie reached back, grabbed my arm, and pulled me to the window.

Daddy climbed out of the truck holding his hand up. It was wrapped in a towel. "Lou Anne?" he called. My sister came rushing out the front door with Missy in her arms.

"Daddy, you all right? What happened?"

"Yeah, I'm all right. I was replacing a broken window and the new pane busted on me. Help me bandage it, wouldya?"

Lou Anne stepped back. "Oh, Daddy, you know I can't stand the sight of blood. It makes me sick."

"Cass!" he bawled. "Cass!" He turned toward Lou Anne. "Where's your sister?"

"Cover for me, Lou Anne," I whispered, hanging on to Jemmie's curtain.

Lou Anne looked flustered. I knew she didn't want to rat on me but Daddy was standing there, waiting. Finally she said, "She's over next door."

"At the Winthrops?" He looked at the house on the other side of ours where the oldest kid was no more than four. "What's she doing there?"

"Not there. Over at Miss Liz's old place."

As Daddy turned, he took off his baseball cap. He leaned back and looked up at the house rising above the fence we'd built. He looked right at me, and at Jemmie who was standing beside me. "Catherine Bodine, you heard me call you," he said quietly. "Get your butt down here. Now."

"Coming, Daddy."

"Ooooh, girl..." Jemmie whispered, "we're in trouble now." She clutched my arm. "I'm coming with you."

"That's not a good idea."

"We're a team, Cass."

We passed Artie and Nana Grace on the porch. "You two be respectful," Nana said. "But hold your heads up. You got nothin' to be ashamed about."

With our linked arms squeezed tight between us, Jemmie and me walked around the fence. It was the first time a Lewis had ever set foot in Bodine territory. "Daddy," I said, "this is our new neighbor, Jemmie Lewis." One look at Daddy's face told me Jemmie wasn't welcome.

"I'm pleased to meet you, sir," Jemmie said, sounding real respectful, just like Nana Grace had told her to.

"You come inside, Cass."

Just then the Lewises' pickup rumbled by and turned in next door. "Sir, I'll be right back with my mother," Jemmie said. "She'll help you. Blood doesn't make her sick. She's a nurse."

It took a minute for Jemmie to convince her mother to come around the fence. When she did, Mrs. Lewis just stood with her white shoes on our dried-up lawn. She glanced at the towel on Daddy's hand, which was soaked through with blood.

"It doesn't look like you'll be building any fences for a while," she said, and crossed her arms. "My daughter says I should look at your hand."

"We can manage."

I touched his arm. "But Daddy, wouldn't it be better to have a real nurse take a look?"

"I said we can handle it, Cass."

"Good," said Mrs. Lewis. "Let's go, Jemmie." She turned on her heel, but there was Mama standing at the edge of the yard. Mrs. Henry's car was pulling away.

Mama clasped her hands and the color drained out of her face. "What's the matter, Seth?"

"Oh, for cryin' out loud," my father said. "I cut my hand is all."

Mrs. Lewis had Jemmie by the arm and was towing her away. By grabbing Jemmie's free arm and one of Mama's, I tried to bring our two mothers together. "Mama, these are the Lewises, our new neighbors."

Mama's glance stuttered from Mrs. Lewis to Daddy and back again. She smiled weakly and nodded. "I'm pleased to meet you, but I need to look after my husband, excuse me." She followed Daddy into the house.

"Well!" Jemmie's mother said. She tightened her grip on Jemmie and steamed off.

Lou Ann followed my parents into the house.

Alone in the yard, I went and sat in my chair. I could hear their voices from the other side of the fence.

"How long have you been spending time with that girl next door?" Mrs. Lewis asked.

"A while. She likes to run. She's fast, too."

"That's beside the point."

"Now, Leona," I heard Nana Grace say, "you couldn't ask for a better friend for your girl. Cass is bright and good-natured. They're friends. Why, them girls are so tight you couldn't slide a buttered knife between 'em."

"But the family...they're a bunch of bigots."

"The child's not responsible for the parents."

"Still, I can't allow our Jemmie to visit with that girl anymore."

"Please, Mom, please," Jemmie begged. "I won't go over to her house, and I won't even say boo to her family. There ain't a thing wrong with Cass."

"I told you, don't say ain't."

"Isn't!" she shouted. "There *isn't* a thing wrong with Cass!"

"I'm sorry, Jemmeal. I'm only trying to do what's best."

"You say *they're* prejudiced? You're just as bad." I heard Jemmie run across the porch. The screen door slammed with such force it bounced, then clattered against the door frame.

"This ain't right, Leona," I heard Nana Grace say.

"Isn't," said Jemmie's mother, but she sounded tired. "And it is right. That girl is being raised by folks who are full of hate. Don't think she isn't picking it up. A friend like that would just drag Jemmie down."

The door opened and closed a second time, but more quietly, as Jemmie's mother followed her inside.

I sat in my chair hugging my stomach. I felt too bad to cry. The only sounds I heard from next door were the rockers of Miss Liz's old chair on the floor boards and Nana Grace singing sad and slow, "Oh the river of Jordan is so wide...one more river to cross."

A while later Mama and Daddy came back out. "I can't get the bleeding stopped," Mama said. "I'm taking Daddy to the emergency room. You better get inside and start supper."

Supper was cold by the time they got home from the hospital. Daddy's hand was in a big white bandage. Just by looking at their faces I could tell it had cost a lot of money. "You okay, Daddy?"

"Thirty-two stitches," he said. He squeezed the back of my neck with his good hand. "You stay away from next door, understand?"

Since Jemmie wasn't allowed to see me anyway, I didn't fight him, but I didn't say, "Yes, Daddy." I felt sorry for him with his hurt hand, but what he was doing, ordering me to stay away from Jemmie, was just plain wrong.

Thirty-two stitches didn't change that.

CHAPTER TEN

A Closed Case

When I woke up the next morning it took a minute for me to remember what had happened. At first I just listened to Lou Anne breathing in her bed across the room and the birds singing outside. The house was filled with a Saturday quiet. Then I remembered. Suddenly I felt achy all over, like I was coming down with the flu.

I got dressed, but I carried my sneakers down the hall so I wouldn't wake anyone up. Then I slipped out of the house. It was already hot and hazy outside.

I walked down the street. Cody Floyd was sitting in the middle of the road in front of his house with a box of sidewalk chalk next to him. His shadow went across the tar and into the grass. "Hey, Cass," he said. "I'm drawing a monster truck rally. Wanna help?"

"No thanks, Cody." I started to jog, but I shouted back at him, "Watch out for cars, okay?"

I was anxious to get to the school. Maybe Jemmie was sitting under the pecan tree waiting for me. Her mother would want her to keep running so she could get that athletic scholarship and grow up to be a doctor. If Jemmie didn't mention I'd be there, her mother wouldn't think twice about letting her go.

But she wasn't there, so I sat under the tree by myself, stretching and still hoping she'd come. Finally, I ran alone, but I didn't run fast. The whole time I was listening for the squeak of the gate and Jemmie's shout, "Get it in gear, girl! Move your butt!" When I finally heard someone coming it was just Ben and Justin and a couple of boys named Nick and John, brothers who lived around the corner from Justin. The basketball made a twanging sound as Ben trotted along dribbling it.

I stopped running and lay down under the tree. I watched a couple of squirrels play tag in the top branches and listened to the boys.

"I can't believe you missed that one," Ben whooped. "Want to get up on my shoulders and try again?" Ben was shooting rings around the other boys, but they were still having a good time. It only made me miss Jemmie more. I tried to think of what to say to Daddy to make him change his mind about her. Jemmie was probably at home right now working on her mother.

Too bad we had to convince the two most stubborn people in the world.

When I got home, Cody was gone, but he had left a nice drawing of one monster truck driving right over the top of another one and all his chalk lying in the road. I put the chalk up on the grass so it wouldn't get run over.

The first thing I saw at my house was Lou Anne stretched out on a towel in the front yard. She was wearing a bikini she and Carey had picked up on sale at the mall. Seeing her in it always made Mama shake her head and tell her to cover up. Lou Anne had a slice of cucumber on each eye.

"Hi, Lou." It was the first thing I'd said to her since the night before.

She lifted a cucumber slice and looked up. "You mad at me, Cass? You know I didn't want to tell on you, but Daddy asked."

I sat down on the ground next to her towel. "Oh, it's okay."

"It is?" She uncovered both eyes and smiled. "Well, thank goodness." She examined the cucumber slices, then flipped them over and set them back on her eyelids.

"Lou Anne, what are you doing?"

"What's it look like?" She lay there with the cucumber slices balanced on her eyelids. "I'm working on my tan."

"I mean with the vegetables."

"I'm soothing the delicate skin around my eyes. Want me to get you a couple slices? There's plenty more in the kitchen."

I appreciated the fact that she was trying to cheer me up, but I had something important to do. "No thanks, Lou. I have to talk to Daddy."

"You sure you want to do that?" She lifted both slices and peeked at me. "He's in no mood, Cass."

As soon as I opened the door, I saw that the TV was on. A couple of men in plaid shirts were catching bass and telling about some kind of miracle lure called the Killer Minnow. All I could see of Daddy was his fat, bandaged hand propped on the back of the sofa. I walked around to his side and sat down on the edge of the coffee table. He was asleep. Even though he worked in the sun all the time, today he was as pale and gray as the cigarette ash in the ashtray beside him. His mouth twisted down.

It's a funny thing. If you look hard for a while at someone you know really well, it seems like you're looking at a total stranger. I looked at him like I'd never seen him before and I wondered, is this what a bigot looks like? And if he is a bigot, when did he become one? Something must have happened when he was young. It must've been pretty bad to make him hate people he didn't even know.

He groaned and opened his eyes.

"Your hand hurt, Daddy?"

"I'll show you where it hurts." With his good hand, he patted the pocket where he kept his wallet.

"Daddy...." I knelt down on the rug beside him so I could look into his eyes. "I need to talk to you about Jemmie, my friend from next door."

"Case is closed on that, Catherine."

"Why?" I asked. "Why is it closed?"

"Because I said so." He rapped his bandaged fist lightly on the back of the sofa. "End of discussion." He burrowed his shoulder into the cushion and closed his eyes.

I smacked the switch on the TV as I left, but he sputtered, "Hey, I was watching that." I turned it back on and stamped out of the room and into the kitchen.

Mama was standing at the sink peeling potatoes. The sun through the window lit up her pale red hair. "Don't be yelling at your father, Cass. He's hurting."

"But he won't listen. I just want to go on seeing my friend. It ain't fair, Mama."

As she put her arm around my shoulders I smelled the talcum powder she always wore. "No," she said, stroking my hair with a damp hand, "life ain't always fair, Cass."

I thought about Nana Grace, about all the unfairness she had seen and how she had outlasted it. I guess I didn't have that much patience. I wanted to see Jemmie now. I took a deep breath. "Would you talk to him, Mama?"

"I'll try," she said, keeping her voice down, "but he's feeling pretty low right now, and it's not just the hand. You remember how he got all excited about that job at the university?"

"I remember." Lou Anne had typed up his application for a job as a maintenance mechanic at one of the dorms. The pay was so much better, Mama had told us to say a little prayer. But we had all been sure he was going to get it. After all, he could fix anything. "Did he hear?"

"Yes. Another man got the job. Either one of them could've done the work, but the other man was black. Your father's sure that that's what tipped the balance."

"Mama?" I said with my cheek against her shoulder, "Is Daddy a bigot like Jemmie's mother says? Does he really hate black people?"

She turned and held me at arm's length, and I thought she was going to say that of course he didn't hate black people, that it was all a big misunderstanding, and that she was going to fix everything. But she didn't.

"I don't know why he feels the way he does," she said. "He learned it at home, I guess. His folks were like that too. The Bodines always had it hard. Maybe it helped them get by, thinking they were better than somebody."

"But that's not right! You have to talk to him. If he got to know Jemmie, he'd like her, I know he would."

She squeezed my shoulders. "Cass, your father's a good man. He works hard to take care of all of us. I'll talk to him, but I don't want to fight with him. I'll try, but I don't think he's going to change."

I could feel my lips trembling. "Jemmie's grandmother says you have to stand up for what's right, no matter what."

Suddenly she looked tired. "I guess I'm not as brave as Jemmie's grandmother," she said softly.

I twisted away from her and ran up to my room. I didn't want to see either one of my parents for a long, long time.

~

I stayed in my room for hours. Nobody noticed but Lou, who snuck me up some lunch, then went right back to working on her tan. I took a nap. I flipped through Lou Anne's beauty magazines. The time passed slower than on a school day. It got to be the middle of the afternoon, and I still didn't feel one bit better. Finally, I left the house.

"Hey, Cass." Ben was riding his bike down the street. He turned and circled around me. "How's it going?"

"Go away, Ben." I didn't want to talk.

He hopped off the bike. The gears went *tick, tick, tick* as we walked along with the bike between us. "What's eating you, Cass?"

I didn't want to tell him, but it didn't seem like he was going to leave me alone. He walked all the way to the graveyard with me, then leaned his bike against the fence. When I climbed up on Henry Hudson's marble box, he did too. We sat cross-legged at opposite ends, quiet for a while. Then he stretched out a leg and nudged me with his bare toes. "Now, you gonna tell me what's wrong?"

"I guess." Tracing the letters on the stone with a finger, I told him about Jemmie and how my father wouldn't let me see her.

"That's tough," he said. He fished a rock out of his pocket and tossed it from hand to hand. "Old people get into habits," he said. "They make their mind up about a thing and they don't ever change."

I looked around at the gravestones, some of them so weathered you couldn't even read them. "Up in heaven, where these folks are, nobody even has skin. Why does it matter so much here?"

"It shouldn't." He pitched the rock as hard as he could to see how far it would go. When it hit the church foundation, he looked satisfied. "When you grow up, you can be friends with whoever you want."

"Like in a million years," I said.

We stretched our legs out so they alternated, his leg, my leg, his leg, my leg. Our legs were just about the same tan, our feet about the same dirty.

"I can see your scar," I said, pointing at the little silver crescent up by his eye. We were only about seven when he got it.

"From when we pretended we were spies," he said.

"That's right, and you said we should squeeze under the Winthrops' hedge."

"Dumb move," he said. "I'd just poked my head out when that old beagle of theirs nailed me." Seeing the scar made me think about how long I've known Ben. Since forever.

After that we just talked. He told me about how he was working on his hook shot. I told him about reading *Jane Eyre* with Jemmie. We talked until our shadows were so long they touched Miss Liz's stone. I listened to the sound of his voice going on and on like it had for as long as I could remember. Hearing it was like getting a drink when you're real thirsty.

"Bet it's coming on supper time," he said at last.

"I guess." I didn't want to go home. I would've rather gone on talking.

We walked to the fence. He stood the bike up, and slung a leg over it. "Well, whaddya waiting for?" He nodded at the handlebars. "A written invitation?"

Until a year ago I rode on his handlebars all the time. Then things got weird. People started saying we were boyfriend and girlfriend. But there was no one to see us now, so I climbed up. My legs had gotten longer, so it was tricky, but I finally got balanced.

"Now hang on good," he said, his voice right in my ear. "We are gonna fly." When he stood on the pedals we wobbled a little. Then he strained forward and I leaned back against him. We picked up speed fast. My head bounced against his collarbone and my hair whipped back over his shoulder. We tore through the warm air like a shooting star.

Lou Anne was just picking up her towel and beauty magazines when we got to my house. "Well, aren't you two a cute couple," she said.

"Shut up," I told her, climbing down.

Ben blushed. "Later, Cass." I watched as he streaked away fast, standing on the pedals.

Mama gave me an anxious look when I walked in, like she had been worrying about where I was. When she filled our plates, she gave me an extra-big helping of my favorite, mashed potatoes.

Even though he couldn't fold his hands, Daddy said his usual grace. "Thank you Lord for food and family." For the rest of dinner, all you could hear was forks clinking.

When the others sat down to watch TV, I went up to my room and flopped down on my bed. I had read every word in my magazines, so I just stared at a double-page picture of runners going single file along the top of a ridge. They looked so free, running like that with the sun setting behind them. I pretended one of them was me and one of them was Jemmie.

Running with Jemmie, reading *Jane Eyre* together, or just sitting on her bed talking all seemed as far away as the ridge in the picture.

CHAPTER ELEVEN

I Find Out about My Ears

L ou Anne came back in from the mailbox. "Look what I got." She dropped a magazine in my lap. "I'll give you first peek. I haven't even looked at the monthly hair tips. Cross my heart, I haven't even opened the cover."

She still felt bad about me and Jemmie and she was trying to be nice, so I took her beauty magazine out to my chair by the fence. Maybe I could use up the last five weeks of summer reading the monthly hair tips.

I sat down, but I forgot all about Lou Anne's magazine. Voices were coming from the other side of the fence. "Let him go, Jemmie. Come to Nana, Artie." It sounded like Artie was taking his first steps, toddling from Jemmie to Nana Grace. "Come to Nana and you can pat the kitty." They were using General Lee for bait. "Good boy!"

"Back to me now, Artie," Jemmie called. She hadn't come to the track that morning or Sunday either—I snuck over before church just to make sure—and I missed her bad. Now that she was so close, I wanted to shout to her, or stare at her through the knothole, but it wouldn't do any good. I knew if I did, I'd only miss her worse.

I spread Lou Anne's stupid magazine across my knees. It opened right up to this month's hair tips. The topic was "Coping With Thin Hair." It had "before" pictures and "after" pictures. I looked just like the "befores."

I went back inside. "Lou Anne, can you fix me like this?" I pointed to one of the "afters."

"Sure," she said. Lou Anne did Carey's hair all the time, and the girls' at the shelter, sometimes even Mama's. Usually, though, she worked on a dummy head she ordered from the back of one of her magazines. She was always glad to get what she called a "living head" to work on.

She sat me on a stool and threw a kitchen towel around my neck. "I can do you one better than this," she said taking a stab at the picture with her comb. "I'm going to give you big hair, like in those beach party movies. It'll be cool."

Because we didn't get cable, Lou Anne and Carey always got stuck watching old movies. I think Lou watched them for the hairstyles. She hummed as she went to work on my living head, raking the comb up and down through my hair.

"What're you doing?"

"It's called teasing."

It hurt almost as bad as Jemmie's braid job.

"Hold still, Cass."

She teased.

She fluffed.

She sprayed.

When I begged her to let me take a look she said, "Not 'til I'm all done. That way you'll get the full effect."

Daddy came home.

"How was your day?" Lou Anne asked, shaking her can of hair spray and giving my head a blast.

"Lousy," he said. "Can't do much with one hand." He opened the refrigerator door and reached for the iced tea pitcher with his good hand. "You spray that hair any more, Lou, it's going to break off."

Mama came home.

"Isn't that hairdo a little old for her, Lou Anne?"

"This is special, like for a party or a dance or something." She tugged at my hair, ratting the back a little more.

"Is Cass going somewhere special?" Mama asked.

Lou Anne gave my hair another coat of spray.

"That style used to be called a beehive," Mama said.

Lou Anne scrunched the sides of my hair in her fists to give it a final lift. "Perfect," she said, "now close your eyes." She grabbed me by the shoulders and steered me to the mirror in the living room. "Open 'em," she said.

When I saw myself, I almost screamed. My hair was stiff and shiny. "I look like Marge Simpson!"

"Oh, you do not. It makes you look at least fifteen, don't you think?"

"More like forty-five."

The only thing that would have made it worthwhile to look like I was wearing a Dairy Queen sundae on my head was if Jemmie could see it.

For a minute I had this crazy idea. I would go out to the fence and center myself in front of the knothole, just like Jemmie had made me do the first time we met. Sooner or later she was bound to walk by and glance through the hole. When she did she would scream with laughter at my blizzard hairdo. Of course I didn't do it, but I could've. It wasn't like I had anything better to do for the rest of the summer.

~

"Your hair!" Lou Anne shrieked when I sat up in bed the next morning. Then she laughed so hard she had to hold on to her stomach.

I scrambled out of bed and over to the bureau. "Oh my gosh." I blinked at the mirror. My hair was squished flat in the back and flared like spread wings on the sides.

"Don't worry." Lou Anne climbed out of bed and stretched, then she walked over to me. She pressed down the sides of my hair, but they just wouldn't stay. "Seems like it's stuck. Too much spray, I guess. Go wash it out. I'll fix it back like it was."

I washed it, then Lou Anne did her best, but even though she brought tears to my eyes, she couldn't comb the knots out. Finally, she laid her comb down. She looked like she was going to cry. "Take me out and shoot me, Cass. I couldn't do worse if I was trying to wreck your summer."

"Stop it, Lou Anne. It looks like you'll just have to give me a haircut."

"I will?" She had only given a trim to the dummy head, not an actual haircut because the dummy had cost her twenty-one dollars plus shipping and the hair wouldn't grow back. Mama didn't let her give haircuts at the shelter.

"Choose your style," she said, flopping open the scrapbook where she kept pictures of Short and Sassy Cuts. I picked one that would stop just below my ears, which was as much hair as she thought she could save.

It turned out Lou Anne had been optimistic. When she was done my hair was as short as baby Missy's.

"Cass...I'm so sorry! I never knew your ears stuck out like that." She pinned them to the sides of my head with her hands, but when she let go they sprang right back. "Are you going to be all right?" She asked, looking miserable.

With my head practically bald and my ears sticking out, I had gone from plain to plain ugly.

"It's only hair, Lou," I said. I left the house fast and waited until I was in my chair by the fence, hidden from the house, then I let go and cried. My shoulders heaved. Tears dripped off my chin and onto my knees. It wasn't just the hair. It was everything. I cried until I gave myself the hiccups.

Through the blur of tears, I saw something white drop from the sky with a slow, loopy flight. It flipped once, then perched in the rose of Sharon.

A paper airplane.

I blotted my eyes with the hem of my shirt and picked it up. It was folded, but I could see it had writing on it. I unfolded it, smoothed the paper flat against my legs, and stared at the big black letters.

DON'T WORRY GIRL
IT'LL GROW BACK

Miss Liz Speaks

Day after day things were just like they were before Jemmie moved in, but they were different too. Before Jemmie, I expected to run by myself. Running alone, I felt like a balloon with nobody holding on to my string. After Jemmie, running alone was just lonely. I missed her hustle-talk. Like when I was tired, Jemmie would say, "What's the matter, girl, you bust a foot? You slow down any more and I'm gonna run up your back and down your front." I even missed watching the soles of her sneakers flash as she sprinted out ahead yelling, "And it's Jemmie Lewis in the lead, Jemmie Lewis going for the gold!"

One afternoon I dropped my running magazines over the fence for her. I missed her that bad. But I kept running because when school started we would still be Chocolate Milk, fastest thing to ever hit Monroe Middle, and I wanted to be ready.

Each day, after running against myself, I went to see Miss Liz and H. H. I put fresh flowers in Miss Liz's pickle jar, lay a couple of blooms on H. H.'s chest like Jemmie had done, then I sat up on the marble sofa and talked to Miss Liz. One day I found a folded-up piece of paper under the pickle jar along with my three running magazines. When I unfolded the piece of paper there was a note on it and the stub of a pencil.

Dear Cass,

This is Miss Liz writing to you NOT Jemmie. She's not allowed. First off she said to thank you for the magazines. She says she'll look for that Zone they talked about. Then she asked me to ask you, is it okay if she finishes Jane Eyre? She can read it, then you can read it, then when you get to school you can talk it over.

p.s. Jemmie figures it will be OKAY to talk to you at school.

p.p.s. She ISN'T going to check it out with her mother.

Sincerely,
Miss Liz

I sat down on the marble sofa to think it over. If Jemmie read *Jane Eyre*, she would know way ahead of me if Jane really did like Mr. Rochester. She would find out the truth about the spooky laughter that woke Jane up in the night at Thornfield Hall. And there was another thing. Jemmie and Jane would be hanging out together without me. Finally I wrote back.

Dear Jemmie,

Cass says you're welcome for the magazines. She's been having a hard time finding The Zone herself.

She says she guesses that it's okay for you to read Jane Eyre by yourself, EXCEPT THE END. You two have to read the end TOGETHER.

p.s. She says to ask, is your mother softening up any?

p.p.s. She says if you're just sitting on your butt she's going to dust you when you two get out on the track again.
Very truly,
Miss Liz.

And that's how we communicated for a while; we left each other notes under Miss Liz's jar. At first Jemmie was giving me hints about Jane Eyre, like

Dear Cass,
Jemmie's not going to tell you if he was in it, but someone set fire to Mr. Rochester's bed.

and

Dear Cass,
Mr. Rochester has a girlfriend. Jemmie's not saying, but it might not be Jane.

Finally Miss Liz wrote her back.

Dear Jemmie,
Quit spoiling Jane Eyre for Cass. If you tell her everything there won't be anything left except looking up the big words. Which she can't because Lou Anne left their dictionary over at Carey's house.

After that Miss Liz just wrote about what Jemmie was up to.

Dear Cass,
Don't you worry about Jemmie getting out of shape. Her mother takes her to the Y

*every night. Jemmie runs while her mom takes
an exercise class. It's cool and comfortable
at the Y, but there are all these old geezers
clogging up the track. They jog with their
elbows out like chicken wings. Jemmie runs
by them so fast she practically blows them
over. She's seen enough old ladies in the
locker room in their underwear to know she
doesn't ever want to get old.
p.s. They look like candles that have
melted all over themselves.
p.p.s. There's nobody at the Y who runs
like you Cass. Just a bunch of foot draggers.*

Jemmie got a nickname at the Y. The geezers and the melted candle ladies called her Wilma. I had Miss Liz write back to ask her why. I didn't think that Wilma Flintstone was much of a runner. Miss Liz wrote back— and she was beginning to sound more like Jemmie all the time.

*Girl,
Don't you read any of those posters they
hang up for black history month? Forget
Wilma Flintstone. They're talking about
Wilma Rudolf the famous track star.*

Then one day, instead of the usual note, Miss Liz's leather bound edition of *Jane Eyre* was there, perched on top of Miss Liz's stone. It had its little satin ribbon marker on the page where Jemmie and me had left off. The last few pages were paper-clipped together. There were so many clips, it looked like the end of the book was wearing braces. I sat down on the marble sofa and started right in. "'For several subsequent days I saw little of Mr. Rochester. In the mornings he seemed much engaged in business.'" I realized that I was reading aloud, but after reading with Jemmie, it seemed like the only way to read *Jane Eyre*. So I read for Miss Liz and Henry Hudson DeWitt and anybody else who hadn't heard a story for a long time and might like one.

If they wanted to know about the beginning, Miss Liz could fill them in.

Jane and Mr. Rochester were having one of their evening chats by the fire. Mr. Rochester, who seemed like he was in a pretty good mood, said he was "disposed to be gregarious." I thought that dispose was when you threw something out, and I didn't know a thing about gregarious. I left a note for Jemmie. It turned out that being disposed to be gregarious just meant that Mr. Rochester liked being with people.

After that I left a list under the pickle jar each day. Seemed like no one but the dictionary knew these words anymore, words like perambulate and importune and salubrious.

According to Jemmie's note, to perambulate is to stroll around. I could use that one when we ran together again. "You think you could you perambulate a little faster?" Importune is like asking for something over and over—nowadays it's called whining. Salubrious is something that makes you feel healthier.

After she wrote the definitions she'd always ask something like, Did Mr. Rochester's bed catch on fire yet? just to see how far along I was.

Little Miss Hitler at the Beach

A breath of cool air blew in the window as I sat up in bed and stretched. "What a salubrious morning."

Lou Anne rolled onto her side. "Sa-loo-bree-us?"

"Yeah, it means the kind of day that makes you feel good." I pounded my chest and did a Tarzan yell.

Lou Anne yelled right along with me. Guess she was feeling salubrious too. She poked her feet out from under the sheet. "Whaddya think?"

"About what?"

She wiggled her toes. "The color." Her nails were painted the same pukey pink as our room. "You think the color brings out my tan?"

"I guess."

She sat up and swung her feet back and forth. "Guess what? Andy's taking me to the beach today."

"Did Daddy say you could go?"

"I didn't ask yet, but he'll say yes. It's Saturday. It's not like I have to watch Missy."

When we went downstairs Daddy was reading the *Tallahassee Democrat* at the breakfast table, and Mama was frying sausage. "Daddy, Mama," Lou Anne said, looking from one to the other, "guess what?"

"What, sweetheart?" Mama looked hopeful, like Lou Anne might announce that she'd just won the lottery.

"Andy Thompson has his daddy's car today, so he's going to take me to the beach, okay?"

Daddy never looked up from the sports page. "Over my dead body."

Mama fluttered over to him. "Now, Seth, let's hear the details before we go making rash decisions." She poured a little more coffee into his cup. "You'll be going with a bunch of the kids, right?"

"Well, no."

I could see the hope in Lou Anne's eyes begin to flicker.

"But you'll be back real early?"

Poor Mama, grasping at straws.

"Actually, his uncle has a condo on Saint George Island. He said we could stay the night."

"Just you two?" Mama said in a strained voice, like someone was squeezing her windpipe.

"Oh, no, Mama. You know his cousin Mike? The one who goes to U. F.? He'll be there. He's twenty-one."

Daddy tipped his chair up on its back legs and asked my mother, "Laura, did you drop this child on her head and forget to tell me about it?" He pointed his fork at Lou Anne. "You tell that Andy if he keeps coming up with funny stuff like that, I'm gonna shoot him next time he comes around."

I wanted to warn Lou Anne not to beg, that around here it didn't help.

Her lips began to quiver. "Oh please, Daddy, please. All I've done all summer is mind the baby and stay home." Tears spilled down her cheeks. "I haven't done one fun thing."

"Now look what you did," Mama said to Daddy. "Here, honey." She grabbed a tissue and held it out to Lou Anne. "Now, we're going to talk all this over. I just know we can come up with a compromise."

I was as disgusted as Daddy, but for a different reason. Mama would hunt for any little compromise so that Lou Anne could smooch around with Andy at the beach. But when I asked if she'd talked to Daddy about Jemmie, she said she hadn't found the right time yet.

I grabbed *Jane Eyre* and headed for my spot. Once I was in my chair I wished I had ear plugs. I could hear Lou Anne and Mama importuning all the way out there.

But as I read, their voices began to fade. I had finally made it to the part about the fire: "Tongues of flame darted round the bed; the curtains were on fire. In the midst of the blaze and vapour, Mr. Rochester lay stretched motionless, in deep sleep."

Mama called, "Oh, Cass honey...we need to talk to you."

Darn. I knew that something would save Mr. Rochester, but for now he would just have to lie there like a hot dog on a grill because Mama and Lou Anne, all smiles, were coming toward me across the lawn.

"Cass?" Mama hung on to Lou Anne's arm. "We've come up with a great compromise. You'll go with Andy and Lou Anne. Now, won't that be fun?"

"Please come, Cass," Lou Anne pleaded. "Pretty please." After all her crying, her eyelashes came to little points.

"Oh, all right," I said. It beat staying home.

～

Andy put his arm around Lou Anne and pulled her toward him across the front seat. "I can't believe you had to bring your bald-headed little sister." He ran his thumb under the shoulder strap of the one-piece swimsuit Mama had made Lou wear as part of the compromise. Then he stomped the gas pedal and the car surged. My shoulder blades dug into the backseat upholstery.

"Put on your seat belt, Lou Anne," I said.

Their heads swiveled toward me. "What?"

"You heard me. Put on your seat belt."

Andy slapped the back of the seat. "I'm going to turn around right now if Little Miss Hitler is going to do this all day."

Lou Anne hissed, "Please, Cass...don't do this to me. I'll just die if I have to spend another boring day at the house. You don't want to go home either, do you?" She slid over and buckled her belt, but she reached across and grabbed Andy's hand.

She was right. A day at the beach—even a day at the beach with Andy—was better than moping around at home. I opened *Jane Eyre* and tried to ignore the front seat.

Jane saved Mr. Rochester from burning. She poured water on him. Then there was a whole long part where Mr. Rochester ran around Thornfield Hall with a candle, figuring things out. When he came back he said the fire was started by the servant, Grace Poole, the one with the crazy laugh, and then he held Jane's hand and thanked her over and over. I think he just wanted to hold her hand.

Meanwhile, in the front seat, Andy was driving one-handed and barely watching the road. I read another page. The next time I looked up, I saw him run his palm over Lou's bare arm. When he gave her shoulder a squeeze, she let out a squeal. It was disgusting. After that I tried not to look.

When we were almost there, Lou Anne pointed out a roadside stand. "I'd just love some boiled peanuts," she said. Andy bought her a bag. She only ate a couple herself, then remembered that peanuts are fattening. After that she just shelled them for Andy and put them in his mouth. He sucked the salt off her fingers.

"Want some?" She offered me the bag over the back of the seat.

"No thanks. Not with Andy's spit on 'em."

We carried armloads of stuff down the wooden walkway to the beach and dropped it in the first clear spot. People were everywhere. Women in bikinis lay on their backs on towels. Fat men stood with the waves slapping their bellies as they cast their fishing lines. Some little kids were building a sand castle. The rising tide was nibbling it away as fast as they could build it.

Lou Anne and me spread our towels out. Andy pulled his T-shirt over his head. Since he had spent most of his summer behind Mr. G.'s counter, his skinny chest was pure white. He said, "Lou Anne, wouldya do my back?" and held out a bottle of sunscreen.

The wind blew Lou Anne's hair across her face. She held it back with one hand, took a look at Andy, and wrinkled her nose. "You don't need sunscreen. You look like you've been under a rock. It wouldn't hurt you to get a little color."

I didn't think that was such a good idea. Without sunscreen Andy Thompson was going to fry worse than Mr. Rochester with his bed on fire, but I didn't want to get called Little Miss Hitler again for saying so. I kept my mouth shut and just put sunscreen on myself.

Andy did put zinc oxide on his nose and cheekbones. When he smeared some on Lou Anne, they looked like a couple of Indians from the same tribe. He was screwing the lid on the jar when she slapped his butt and sprinted for the water. "Bet you can't catch me!" She slowed down just enough to make sure he could. He swept her up in his arms, then staggered. I thought for sure he was going to drop her. If she toppled him, Lou Ann would never talk about anything but her fat thighs ever again.

Luckily, he made it to the water. In a minute I could just see their heads bobbing and Lou Anne's shiny, wet arms around his neck, and then they were kissing. If Jemmie was along we'd have laughed at those two—then forgotten all about them. Together we would swim out past the line of people who were jumping the waves, out to where the sea just swelled like it was taking a deep breath.

I swam by myself for a while, out and in. I chased a floating bucket for one of the nearby kids, then I lay on my towel and read. Mr. Rochester's girlfriend arrived at Thornfield Hall along with a whole bunch of other people who seemed to do nothing but sit around being snooty. The girlfriend's name was Blanche. Blanche could sing and play the piano and speak French. Blanche was beautiful. Jane didn't like her. I didn't either. Now, even though Jane had saved him from barbecuing, Mr. Rochester paid no attention to her, he just flitted around this Blanche person. Disgusting. I put the book down and lay on my back.

I pretended that if I looked over at the other towels Jemmie would be there, Jane too; not the Jane who was all interested in Mr. Rochester, but Jane when she was still at the orphanage. She would be in a swimsuit. Definitely a one-piece. She would blink her watery blue eyes and look around at the sunbathers, never having seen so much flesh before in her life. She would be skinny and pale as a peeled twig, her hair parted in the middle. She'd sit quietly on her towel hugging her bony knees.

Jemmie would be lying on her belly, her knees bent, her feet waving around in the air. "Girl," she would say, looking up at Jane, "you ever try Foaming Fizz Powder?"

Jane would shake her head gravely.

"No?" Jemmie would act like she couldn't believe such ignorance. "Well, stick out your hand." Jane would stare at the glittery powder on her palm, wondering what to do with it. "Go on, lick it up." Jemmie and me would both laugh at the shocked expression on Jane's face as the candy hissed inside her mouth.

Of course Jane wouldn't know how to swim. In her day, I don't think it had been invented yet. We would have to teach her. At first each of us would take one of her hands to keep her from getting washed away, but she would catch on quick. Jane was spunky.

I heard a rattling sound and sat up. Jemmie and Jane weren't there, of course, just a seagull trying to steal a chip from the open bag Andy had left on his towel. The gull squawked at me, snatched a chip, and hopped a few feet away to eat it. The closest I could get to Jemmie and Jane was the book, so I went back to reading about Jane at gloomy old Thornfield Hall.

The girlfriend and all the other visitors hung around for a fortnight. I didn't know how long that was, but it was long enough for them to ride around on horses and drink wine and play card games and make Jane, who sat in a corner knitting the whole time, totally miserable.

"Race you to the towels!" Lou Anne yelled as she and Andy came splashing out of the water. Andy looked like a boiled lobster.

"You better put some of that sunscreen on," I said.

He stretched out on his towel. "Who asked you?"

Seemed like Andy would rather fry than do anything Little Miss Hitler told him to.

We ate the lunch Mama had packed: baloney sandwiches with pickles and chips. Lou Anne and Andy fell asleep with Lou's hand on his back. I lay on my stomach to shade the page and went on reading. It turned out that Mr. Rochester's girlfriend, Blanche, wasn't his girlfriend after all. He was only trying to make Jane jealous. This seemed like a pretty mean trick to me, but then I read that he planned to make it up to Jane by marrying her. Marrying her? I slammed the book shut and waded into the water.

It was five-thirty when we shook out the towels and got ready to go. Andy practically glowed. His red back had a paler pink shape, like a jelly-fish on it, where Lou's hand had blocked the sun while they slept. Gritty and salty, we got in the car to head for home.

"Put your seat belt on," I said to Lou Anne.

"It *is* on."

I had to unbuckle my own so I could take a look. "You have that so loose, if we hit anything it's going to jerk you back after you smack the windshield."

"You said to put my seat belt on, so I put my seat belt on." She nuzzled up to Andy, but all he did was wince. He was so burnt, the only place she could've touched him without hurting him was his nose. The zinc oxide had done its job.

Because I didn't want to watch the front seat, I went back to reading. Jane and Mr. Rochester almost got married. Jane had her dress and everything ready. But the night before the wedding she woke up. There was a strange, ghoulish woman in her room trying on her veil. The woman turned and stared at her, then tore the veil in half, threw it on the floor, and stomped on it.

Jane should've known that was a bad sign. But the next day she stuck something else on her head and she walked up the aisle with Mr. Rochester as planned. Everything was fine until they got to the part where the minister asked if anyone knew a reason why the couple couldn't be married. A voice from the back of the church said, "The marriage cannot go on: I declare an impediment."

And what an impediment! Mr. Rochester was already married!

That's when I found out that all the laughing in the night and the bed burning and the veil ripping were done not by the strange servant Grace Poole, but by Mr. Rochester's crazy wife, Bertha. The wife he kept locked in the attic!

Mr. Rochester begged Jane to stay anyway. She told him she would think about it, but deep down she knew it would be wrong. Before daylight she tiptoed down the hall of the mansion. When she got to Mr. Rochester's door she hesitated. She could hear him prowling around in his room, restlessly waiting for morning. She glided by so quietly he never even heard her.

With nothing but the clothes on her back, she left Thornfield Hall. It took all her money to pay for a carriage. When the carriage dropped her off, Jane Eyre was homeless and penniless and heartbroken. But she still had her spunk—and about a hundred pages to go.

I hoped she'd use them to do something interesting. Like join the circus.

Midnight. The Cemetery. Be There.

Andy blew up like a balloon and missed three days of work. "My poor, poor baby," Lou Anne whimpered into the phone, even though she was the reason the poor baby got burned in the first place.

She got burned, too, but not as bad. Because of the zinc oxide she had a pale nose and two light stripes on her cheeks, which drove her crazy. "I'll drop out before I'll go back to school looking like this," she announced. She put sunscreen all around those spots then laid in the sun trying to even things out.

Lou Anne's summer didn't seem to be going any better than mine, so while she worked on her tan I watched the baby. Missy was starting to sit. She couldn't sit up by herself, but if you propped her up a little she could balance like that for a while. She seemed to enjoy seeing the world from a new angle. Her eyes went from thing to thing like she was making a list of everything there was in the world, shiny things especially, and anything that moved.

While she practiced sitting, I read *Jane Eyre* to her. Sometimes when I glanced up she would be slumped over funny. I'd sit her back up, then go on reading.

Jane had hit a real tough spot. She was like the people who wait for the homeless shelter on Tennessee Street to open each evening. Only, in Jane's day there was no homeless shelter. Jane was sleeping on the ground and weak with hunger. She walked to a town, but everyone looked at her funny when she asked if she could have a job or a piece of bread.

She was about to faint when she finally knocked on the right door. Behind that door lived Diana, Mary, and their brother, St. John Rivers. They took her in like a stray dog and they kept her. The brother, St. John, was a missionary, handsome but boring. While Jane recovered he made her learn to speak Hindustani. When she was pretty good at it, and healthy again, he asked her to marry him so they could work side by side in the mud in India until they died of some disease, which was what St. John Rivers said was God's plan for them.

I slammed the book down. Missy flopped over with her blue eyes wide. As I sat her back up I told her, "I didn't read 384 pages just to see Jane go off with an old creep like St. John Rivers." I had to admit that I was beginning to miss Mr. Rochester. He really loved Jane, and not because God told him to either.

Jane missed him too. But page after page, St. John Rivers was wearing her down. She was about to give in and say yes when she heard, clear as anything, a voice calling, "Jane, Jane, Jane!"

"Guess whose voice it was, Missy?" Missy punched the air with her clenched fists as I read to her. "'It was the voice of a human being—a known, loved, well-remembered voice—that of Edward Fairfax Rochester; and it spoke in pain and woe, wildly, eerily, urgently.'" A thrill stabbed my chest. "What do you think of that, Missy?"

And Jane answered back, "I am coming! Wait for me!" and ran into the garden looking for him. Outside, she found nothing but the wind sighing in the trees; the wind, and loneliness, and a "midnight hush." I turned the page quick.

"No!" I shouted. I had run into the paper clips. There were three more weeks before school started.

I tried to figure out what it could mean, Mr. Rochester's voice calling Jane's name so clearly. "Maybe he's dead," I whispered to Missy. "Stuff like that happens. It's in the headlines at the grocery store checkout all the time—voices from beyond the grave, messages from Elvis." Missy blew a spit bubble.

It would be three weeks before I knew if Mr. Rochester was dead or alive. I couldn't wait that long.

Next morning Miss Liz left a note for Jemmie.

> *Dear Jemmie,*
> *Cass says she'll bust if she doesn't find out how the book ends. School is just too far away.*

The answer I got back made my heart pound.

> *Dear Cass,*
> *Jemmie says how do you think she felt waiting for you to catch up with her? Midnight tonight meet her by your old chair, then you two can come here to the graveyard and finish the book together.*
> *p.s. Jemmie has a flashlight, but another one wouldn't hurt.*

I found a flashlight in a drawer in the kitchen. The batteries were so weak it barely glowed. I hid it under my pillow anyway.

When it was time for bed, I slipped my nightgown over my shorts and T-shirt. I didn't want to go bumping around in the dark trying to get dressed. I even kept my sneakers on. I looked pretty lumpy, so I covered myself with a blanket. "Aren't you hot?" Lou Anne asked, walking in from the bathroom brushing her hair.

"I'm fine," I said, sweating under the covers.

I decided the only way I could be sure to be wake up at midnight was not to sleep at all. From my bed I could see the silvery face of Lou Anne's alarm clock. I kept wondering if it was broken, the minute hand moved so slow.

At eleven the stairs sighed; Mama and Daddy were coming up to bed. Like always the third step creaked, the water ran in the bathroom, then the light shining under my door winked out.

I began to drift, spinning down and down like a falling leaf. I jolted awake. The clock only said 11:10. I sat up and looked out the window by my bed.

Moonlight fell like a silky dust on the street. General Lee was walking down the middle of the road, tail switching. He sat down on the stripe, and licked his paw. Frogs *tha-rump*ed. In the distance a train clanged along the track and whistled at the crossing. I wondered if Jemmie was sitting up in her bed looking out into the night too, listening to the train pass.

A hundred years later, when the clock said 11:50, I slid out of bed and tucked *Jane Eyre* under my arm. The old leather cover felt soft and warm. I slid the flashlight out from between the sheet and the pillow and stuck it in my back pocket. Lou Anne sighed, rolled onto her back, and said, "natural blond," clear as a bell, but she was just talking in her sleep.

I walked to the door and opened it slowly. The hinges moaned. I froze and listened for Lou Anne's even breathing. "You look wonderful!" she muttered, probably talking to Carey. Inch by inch I crept out and closed the door behind me.

From behind Mama and Daddy's door I could hear a murmur. They were still awake. My heart clenched. For a minute I couldn't move, but Jemmie was waiting for me. Remembering Jane Eyre leaving Thornfield Hall, I glided down the hall. I slid my hand along the stair rail and felt for each new step with my toes. I did fine until the third step. I remembered too late about the squeak, so, *chirrup!* the stair complained.

I knew Daddy must've heard. In a minute he'd bust out of his bedroom door. And if he didn't come right away it only meant he was putting his pants back on, going for the gun in the nightstand. I stood as still as if my feet were part of the step, but the door never opened. Finally, at snail speed, I went down the last two steps and across the living room.

"Oh, no," I whispered. I had forgotten all about the bolts and chains Daddy had put on the door because he said you never knew who might be prowling around at night looking for an easy target. The chains made little tinkling noises, and the bolts groaned. I opened the front door just enough to slide out.

In the moonlight everything in the yard stood in pools of shadow. I looked across to the fence. I could see the fat shape of the rose of Sharon, but I couldn't see if Jemmie was behind it. While I stood on the step trying to see her I heard a whisper.

"Girl, it's gonna be morning before you make up your mind to get down them steps." And there she was, with one foot on the bottom stair looking up at me.

"Thought you were going to be behind the bush," I said.

"I got tired of waitin' back there." Then she held her flashlight under her chin, switched it on, and gave me a ghoulish grin.

"You look like a skeleton," I said.

"And you look like Mr. Rochester's crazy wife." She pointed to the nightgown I'd forgotten to take off.

"Shoot." I pulled it over my head, crumpled it up, and took it over to the rocking chair behind the bush. Then we just stood there.

It was funny to see Jemmie again. It felt like the first day of school when you see someone after not seeing them all summer, and you're glad to be with them but you don't know what to say. I punched her arm. "Let's see how fast you got running with the old ladies, Wilma."

We took off running down Magnolia, fast at first, but soon we slowed down. The air felt thick as flannel.

"Mr. Barnett is awake," I whispered, looking up at his lighted bedroom window. "He says his bad shoulder keeps him up nights. And there's Cody's bike lying right in the road." I trotted it over to the grass and laid it down. "Looks like he has a flat, too."

We turned the corner. As we jogged single file a car caught us in its headlights. It slowed way down like the driver was looking us over, and I thought about all those guys prowling the night looking for easy targets.

Jemmie must have been thinking the same thing. "Cass," she hissed, "if that guy stops, you and me are going to show him how fast Chocolate Milk can run." But the car moved on.

We got our sneakers and socks wet running through the tall grass of the vacant lot. We could see the faint glow of the marble stones inside the fence. Jemmie rattled the gate. "Locked," she said. "Looks like we gotta vault it."

She went first, running at the gate, then grabbing the bar just below the spikes to boost herself up and over.

"The old ladies teach you that?" I asked as I passed her the book and both flashlights between the iron bars of the fence. I made it over too, but I scraped my thigh on a spike.

The moon shone full between the arching branches of the oaks. H. H.'s marble box glittered like a sugar cube as we took our seats. Jemmie opened the book. She pulled the paper clips off one by one, like she was opening the envelope to announce the next Miss America. When she was finished, I pointed the flashlight at the new page and Jemmie began to read. "'I left Moor House at three o'clock p.m. and soon after four I stood at the foot of the signpost of Whitcross, waiting the arrival of the coach which was to take me to distant Thornfield.'" Jemmie elbowed me. "Looks like Jane's goin' home," she said.

Jane decided to walk the last two miles. The whole way she was wondering if Mr. Rochester would be there, and whether or not she would have the courage to say hey to him if he was. "Well, I hope she don't lose her nerve now," Jemmie said.

Jane just hoped that Mr. Rochester would be looking out a window and see her. "Bet I know how it's gonna go," said Jemmie, passing me the book. "He's gonna run at her, she's gonna run at him, then they're gonna kiss, real real slow."

She pointed to the spot where she had left off and I started reading. "'I looked with timorous joy towards a stately house; I saw a blackened ruin.'" All I got out was that one sentence before Jemmie grabbed the book back.

"What's this trash about a blackened ruin?" She ran her finger along the lines in the book to find her place, then read, "No roof, no battlements, no chimneys—all had crashed in.'" Jemmie shined the flashlight in my face. "Thornfield Hall burned down, Cass."

"No joke." I snatched the book back. "But what about Mr. Rochester?"

There was no way for Jane to guess what had happened to the people who had once lived in the ruined building. To find that out, she rushed back to town, to the local inn. The innkeeper knew all about it but he took his time telling her. First he had to tell her about the crazy wife in the attic, and even about how Mr. Rochester had fallen in love with a governess, which was Jane herself. Jemmie was getting impatient. "Yeah, yeah, yeah," she said, "we know all that. But what happened to Mr. Rochester?"

It took two whole pages for the innkeeper to get around to telling Jane about the night of the fire. He had seen the whole thing himself—the crazy wife standing on the roof, shouting to be heard above the roaring fire, her black hair streaming against the flames. He had seen Mr. Rochester climb up to the roof to get her, but as he walked toward his crazy wife, she jumped. "'And the next minute she lay smashed on the pavement.'"

Jemmie shined the flashlight on her own startled face. "Was she dead?"

I grabbed the flashlight, then pointed to the words. "The innkeeper tells Jane that Bertha was 'dead as the stones on which her brains and blood were scattered.'"

"That sounds pretty dead," Jemmie said. "But what about Mr. Rochester?"

When the innkeeper wrung his hands and declared, "Poor Mr. Edward!" Jane's heart stopped cold. She was sure he was dead. We were sure too.

But no, he was alive, barely, and the innkeeper assured Jane that most folks thought he would be better off dead.

"What's he mean by that?" Jemmie asked.

Mr. Rochester had stayed in the burning building until everyone else had gotten out, which was too long. As he was coming down the great staircase the walls of Thornfield Hall fell around him. When he was dragged out from under the ruin one of his eyes had been knocked out of his head and one hand crushed so bad it had to be cut off. "Ga-ross," Jemmie said.

"Do you think Jane'll stick by Mr. Rochester now that he's blind and missing a hand?" I asked Jemmie.

"Sure I do. She loves him."

Jemmie was right. Jane begged the innkeeper to help her hire a carriage to take her to him. She walked the last mile through a light rain, arriving just as the narrow front door of Ferndean Manor was slowly opening. A figure came out into the twilight, a man who stretched out his hand to feel whether or not it was raining.

"It's Mr. Rochester," Jemmie whispered.

"And he can't see her," I whispered back.

But Jane could see him, "'Dusk as it was,'" I read, "'I recognized him; it was my master, Edward Fairfax Rochester, and no other.'" A wind rattled the oak leaves as if Miss Liz and all the other dead listeners were crowding in close to hear what would happen next, but when he held out his hand in the darkness, Jane stayed out of reach.

"Now why'd she do that?" Jemmie asked.

Jane let him go back in the house without ever knowing she was there, then she went inside and greeted the servants, John and Mary. When Mr. Rochester called out for a drink of water, it was Jane who handed it to him. He heard her voice. He couldn't believe it was really her. He grabbed her hand. "'Her very fingers,'" he cried; "'her small, slight fingers! If so there must be more of her.'" He swept the whole rest of her into his arms.

"'I was entwined and gathered to him,'" Jemmie read, leaning against me, and then she heaved a big sigh and said, "How romantic!" I pinched her hard, even though I thought so too.

Mr. Rochester was ecstatic to be with Jane again, but he was embarrassed too, because he knew he looked bad. Jane could tell that since the fire he'd spent most of his time feeling sorry for himself. "'Am I hideous, Jane?'" he asked, and she said, "'Very, Sir; you always were, you know.'"

"Got to hand it to Jane," Jemmie said. "She'd rather get Mr. Rochester mad than let him throw himself a pity party."

And he did get mad—jealous too. When she told him about St. John Rivers and his offer to take her away to India as his wife, Mr. Rochester got all huffy and ordered her to leave and go back to the man she loved, this St. John Rivers. It took a page and a half for Jane to convince him that she didn't love stuffy old St. John Rivers. The only one she loved was Mr. Rochester himself.

It was my turn to read when Jane Eyre said, "'Reader, I married him,'" like she was talking right to Jemmie and me. And when the wind sighed, I knew that Miss Liz had heard it too, and that she was satisfied.

Jane and Mr. Rochester had a quiet little wedding; no cake or flowers or anything, but they were so happy they didn't even miss those things.

Time flew in the final two pages. One day Mr. Rochester could see out of his one eye again. Jane had a baby boy. St. John Rivers died in the mud in India. It seemed like with each paragraph Jane was walking away from Jemmie and me, growing older and older, striding through the years without once looking back at us. And then the book ended.

Jemmie turned off the flashlight, and we just sat. The wind shivered the oak leaves. The moonlight made each stone glow like a spirit standing in the grass. "I sure am gonna miss that girl," Jemmie said.

"Me too."

"I don't even mind that she married Mr. Rochester."

"Me neither. He was the only one who liked her the way she was."

Jemmie pulled her feet up and hooked her heels over the edge of the marble box. She hugged her shins. "Maybe when school starts we can get another book," she said.

"By the same writer," I said. "We already know what all the hard words mean."

"Cass?" Jemmie put her chin down on her knees and looked off toward the church. "Will things be different when school starts?"

"What do you mean, different?"

"Will we still be friends?"

"Of course we'll be friends. We're Chocolate Milk, remember?"

"You got any other black friends?"

"Not really."

"Kids are gonna say stuff about us."

"We're not gonna let that stop us."

"We're not gonna to let anything stop us," she said, but she didn't sound as sure as usual. "Come on," she said. "Let's perambulate." And we did what we always did when something bothered us. We ran, this time for home, with Jemmie first, and me at her heels.

We were afraid we'd find the lights on at our houses and maybe even a police car or two out front, but both places were dark. As we stood in the street General Lee smoothed around our ankles in figure eights, like a rope tying us together.

"See you in three weeks," Jemmie said.

"Three weeks."

She walked me over to the rose of Sharon bush so I could get my night-gown. Then she thumped her knuckles on the rough fence boards. "Sure is solid."

"Sure is," I said as she disappeared around the end of the fence, going back to her own side.

I made it to bed okay. No one woke up. I was pulling my nightgown over my head when Lou Anne said, "I do." Guess she was dreaming about her wedding again. And her dream wedding wasn't any quiet little *Jane Eyre* event, that's for sure. Her plans included six bridesmaids in seafoam blue and a white stretch limo. "You may now kiss the bride," Lou Anne said, and she puckered up. Bet it was lobster boy giving her that dream-wedding kiss. Lou Anne deserved someone better than Andy, I thought. Someone who would love her more than life itself.

Someone like Mr. Rochester.

The Heat Prostration

"Cass, did you sleep all right?" Mama asked as she filled Daddy's coffee cup. "You have bags under your eyes."

"Try the cucumbers," Lou Anne said. "They really work."

Daddy's newspaper rattled as he turned the page. "S'posed to hit ninety-eight today. And I'm gonna be up cleaning gutters."

"Be sure you wear your hat and drink plenty," Mama said.

It was already too hot when I ran after breakfast. The pecan leaves hung limp and the track shimmered as heat rose off it. I jogged around it once, red dust puffing around my ankles, and then gave up. Walking back, the only flowers I could find looked too droopy to bring to Miss Liz, so I went home without a visit.

Because it was close to the air conditioner, Lou Anne and me spent most of the day on the sofa. The AC won't do the whole house, but if you keep the door to the kitchen closed, the living room stays nice and cool. We ate lunch on the sofa. We painted our toenails and read our horoscopes on the sofa. We let Missy nap on the sofa while we sat next to her and watched show after show.

"Our subject is betrayal," one talk show host breathed into her mike. "Let's meet Heather." A woman with bleached blond hair came onstage and told about how her boyfriend, Bobby, had betrayed her with her best friend, Linda. "And now, let's meet Bobby." Bobby trotted out looking like he was going to win an all-expenses-paid vacation. Heather smacked him.

Then came the best friend, Linda. The audience booed. Heather smacked her too.

While Heather and Linda swung at each other, Lou Anne was looking Bobby over. "Give it up, girls," she said. "He's not worth it."

I dozed off. When I woke up again, a different host was reuniting twins separated at birth. Lou Anne and Missy were gone. It was time for Andy Thompson's 4:30 break. Lou Anne was probably licking a Popsicle right now. Giving away Popsicles was one of Andy's job benefits.

Suddenly, I wanted a Popsicle worse than anything in the world. Andy wouldn't give me one for free, of course, but I had my allowance.

Outside, the heat took my breath away. The only thing that kept me going was imagining that Popsicle. It seemed to float a little way ahead of me as I walked along.

I was still a block from the USA store when I heard Lou Anne yelling and the baby crying. "What do you mean she's been calling you?" Lou Anne screeched. "Why would Tiffany Barlow call you up?"

As I walked up to the store parking lot, I could see Andy leaning against a parked car, trying to look casual. Lou Anne was right in his face. "I can't believe you'd betray me with Tiffany Barlow! She has such limp hair!"

"She's just a friend, Lou Anne. And her hair's not all that limp."

"Oh, so you've been looking at her hair!"

Andy held up his hands. "She's a friend. That's all. We talk, period."

"Talk?" Lou Anne had Missy on her hip, but she didn't seem to notice the baby, even though Missy was crying and crying. "You talk about me, don't you? You and that weasel-faced Tiffany Barlow!"

Andy stared at the ground. His face was peeling so bad that he looked like a mummy with its bandages falling off.

If I were Lou Anne, I would pay Tiffany Barlow to take him.

"Well?" She tapped her foot. "What do you have to say for yourself?"

I slipped into the store.

Mr. G. was hovering like a trapped bug at the window. "They have been bickering for half an hour," he reported. "I went out once to simply suggest to Andrew that his break was over but I could not be heard above the shouting." He pressed his palms together and wagged his fingertips at me. "I have seen this many times. She is a monsoon, your sister. She cannot be stopped. She must rain herself out. Then all will be as it was before."

I slid the freezer door open. I knew exactly what I wanted, but I wasn't in a hurry to get it. I let the freezing fog puff into my face while Mr. G. announced the fight. "Andrew has just covered his face with his arms. Your sister is hitting him. Mercy me! Now she is scratching."

She was acting just like talk-show Heather, and Andy wasn't worth it either.

I had just grabbed a Fudgesicle, the coldest one from the very back, when Mr. G. said, "You know, Cass, the baby is too red. She has no hat and she has been out in the beating sun for a long time. You must look and see."

I paid Mr. G., threw the Fudgesicle wrapper in the trash, and went out.

Lou Anne was still yelling, but Missy had stopped crying. She seemed awful quiet considering all the shouting going on around her. And like Mr. G. said, her face was red as a beet.

"Give her here, Lou," I said.

Lou Anne passed Missy to me like she was an arm load of dirty laundry. "And another thing," she yelled, tugging at the ring on her finger, "you can just take back this old five-dollar Wal-Mart ring. Turns my finger green."

I held the Fudgesicle so it wouldn't drip on the baby, but I didn't take a single lick. I could tell by the way her arms and legs hung that something was really wrong with Missy. I had to get her home, quick as I could. I dropped the Fudgesicle on the ground and began to run.

I could feel her heat clear through my T-shirt. The funny thing was, her skin was dry, not sweaty. I kept glancing down at her. The more I looked, the more scared I got. When her head flopped back I pressed her to my chest and ran harder. "Hold on, Missy." With every step she jounced against me, but she didn't squirm like she usually did when I gave her a tight hug. She hardly moved at all.

I was shaking so hard when we got to the house I couldn't make my key work in the lock. The door opened suddenly and we fell into the house. I practically threw Missy onto the sofa. She still didn't cry.

I didn't know what to do, except that I had to bring her temperature down. I took her top off and her stretchy leggings. She was so limp it was like undressing a doll. When she lay there in just her diaper I could see her chest fluttering up and down. She was breathing way too fast. I set her on the end of the sofa by the air conditioner, but I could see it wasn't enough. Her eyes were wandering but she didn't seem to see anything. For a moment she went stiff. Her back arched and her arms shot up.

"Missy!" I cried.

Then from outside I heard the rattle of the Lewises' truck pulling into Jemmie's yard. Jemmie's mother! She had just spent the day at the hospital helping sick babies. Even though she hated me and all the Bodines, I had to make her help me.

"Mrs. Lewis," I yelled as I ran out of the house. "Mrs. Lewis..."

She had a bag of groceries in her arms, and the truck door was still open.

"Please, please, you've got to come." I tried to snatch the bag out of her arms, I tried to drag her by the arm. She looked at me like I was crazy.

"Leona!" Nana Grace, who was sitting on the porch, stood up so quick she almost knocked Miss Liz's rocker over. "Leona, listen to her. Tell us, Cass, what's the matter?"

"It's the baby. Please, you've gotta come. My baby sister's burning up, and she's real floppy. I think she has the heat prostration."

"The baby?" Jemmie's mother said. That was the first time I saw the little wrinkle she gets between her eyebrows when she's worried. She threw the bag into the truck and groceries spilled across the front seat, but she didn't notice. "Call 911!" she shouted to Nana Grace, then we both ran to my house.

She swept Missy up in her arms and dashed into the kitchen. She turned on the cold water full blast.

"Cass!" Jemmie called. She whipped the screen door open so fast it smacked the wall. "Cass, what's going on?"

"It's Missy. Lou Anne had her out in the sun too long. Now she's really sick."

We could hear the water splashing into the sink and Mrs. Lewis murmuring, "That's it, that's it, come back to me, baby."

Jemmie and I crowded the kitchen door, then held back. We stood with our arms around each other's waists, watching Mrs. Lewis bathe Missy in cool water and beg her to come back.

In the street a car door slammed. "Mama," I whispered. Everything seemed to be moving so slowly, I felt like I was floating as I walked to the front door. Mama had just climbed out of Mrs. Henry's car. She was leaning on the door, talking to her friend through the open window. "I'll bring you that recipe tomorrow, Beth. It's the easiest thing in the world." Mama was smiling when she turned and saw me through the screen door. "Don't let the cool out, Cass, honey," she called. I felt sorry for her. As far as she knew, everything was fine.

"Mama," I said, stepping out onto the stoop, "Mama, Missy's sick. She's in the kitchen with Jemmie's mother."

"Sick?" All the pink drained from her face. She nearly knocked me over getting into the house. The rubber soles of her shoes squeaked as she came to a stop on the kitchen linoleum. Her hands were clenched at her sides. "What's wrong with my baby?" she demanded.

Jemmie's mother glanced up. "She's severely overheated. An ambulance is on its way."

"An ambulance!" Mama moaned, "My baby, oh my sweet baby."

Jemmie's mother cupped Missy's head in her hand and let the cool water run over her.

"She *will* be all right, won't she?" Mama asked. She ran a finger along Missy's cheek lightly, as if she was afraid she might hurt her. "Tell me, please."

Mrs. Lewis didn't answer right away. She fished the stethoscope out of the deep pocket of her smock, closed her eyes, and listened to Missy's heartbeat. Then she opened her eyes and looked at Mama. "I think so," she said at last.

"You think so?" Mama's head bowed until it touched Mrs. Lewis's shoulder. The wail of the ambulance siren jerked it back up again.

"They're here," Jemmie shouted.

The front of Mrs. Lewis's blouse was soaked, and water dripped off her elbows when she pressed Missy up against her chest and raced to the front door. Mama stepped on the back of Mrs. Lewis's shoe, she was following so close.

The light on the ambulance roof wheeled. Two paramedics jumped out of the cab and held the back doors open.

Daddy's truck skidded into the yard. "Laura," he yelled at my mother. "Laura, what's goin' on here?" He jumped out of the truck.

He reached the back of the ambulance just in time to see Jemmie's mother reach out a hand to Mama and pull her inside.

～

Nana Grace looked down at Jemmie and me sitting side by side on the front stoop. "Why don't you two come back over to the house and have some supper?"

"No thank you, ma'am. I'm not hungry," I said.

"Me neither," Jemmie said.

"Nothin' you can do to help by settin' there." Nana jiggled Artie up and down in her arms to quiet him.

"We know," Jemmie said, "but we'd rather wait here."

Nana Grace walked away with Artie tugging at her blouse. I started to cry, thinking about how Missy used to do that to my shirt when I carried her around.

"She'll be okay," Jemmie said fiercely, slinging her arm around my shoulders. "My mother's the world's best nurse, and babies are her specialty."

I felt a little better, then I remembered that one of the first things I ever heard Mrs. Lewis say was that she had lost a baby. Lost meant dead. I thought about the tiny baby graves in Miss Liz's cemetery; the ones with the lambs on them. I pressed my face to my knees.

"Cass, did I ever tell you what made me want to run?"

Even though I knew she was just trying to distract me, I snuffed and dried my eyes on the shoulder of my shirt. "No."

"My dad. He was a runner too, the best in his high school. Even after he left school he still ran. One morning when I was about nine, he woke me up. He put his finger on his lips to tell me to be quiet, then he said to get dressed and put on my sneakers because we were going running. The next morning I was dressed and waiting for him. We ran almost every day before he got sick." She dug her fingers into my shoulder and hung on. "I remember the way he looked. The sun would be coming up. It lit up his white T-shirt and sneakers like he was on fire."

We leaned against each other, silent and numb. We sat and we sat and still they didn't come back. The sun caught in the top of the live oak across the street, starting to go down for the night. It seemed like hours since the ambulance had torn out of the driveway with Daddy's pickup tailgating it. If everything was really okay, why didn't they come back, or call?

Down the street, Cody's bike bell jangled. The sound was faint, but getting louder. "Hey," he said as soon as he could see me, "want to see a trick?" He put his feet up on the handlebars. The bike wobbled all over the place.

"Don't hurt yourself, Cody." I had to squeeze my eyes tight for a second. Missy might never get to ride a bike.

Cody straightened up. "I never hurt myself. Like my tie?" He wore a blue necktie that flapped against the front of his T-shirt. "It's Ben's, for church." He pedaled in big circles. "Who's your friend?"

"This is Jemmie," I said.

"Hi, Jemmie. My name is Cody Floyd. I'm five, going on six. Like my tie?"

"Nice to meet you, Cody Floyd. Why're you wearing a tie? You got a date?"

Cody snorted. "Nuh-uh. Girls stink." He showed us his trick one more time, then pedaled away with the tie waving good-bye over his shoulder.

"Did your father think you were a good runner?" I asked Jemmie.

"He bragged about me all the time, even though my mother told him that doing well in school was the most important thing. He taught me how to play basketball, too. You would've liked him, Cass."

But I wasn't going to get a chance to like him because he was dead. I crossed my arms on my knees and put my head down again.

After a while, Jemmie poked me in the ribs. "Look, here comes your sister."

I rubbed my eyes and nose on the back of my hand. Lou Anne was wandering up Magnolia with a dreamy look on her face. Andy's five-dollar Wal-Mart ring was back on her finger.

"Lou Anne!" I yelled.

"What are you all worked up about, Cass?"

"Missy's at the hospital! You were so busy chewing out Andy you never noticed she was overheating. Now she might die!"

Lou Anne stopped in the middle of the street. "What do you mean, die?"

When I didn't answer, she covered her mouth with both hands. Tears ran down her face.

"Stop it," I said. "Stop it. Crying won't help."

"Come on, Cass. Can't you see how bad she feels?" Jemmie asked me. Then she scooted closer to me and patted the stoop beside her. "Have a seat, Lou Anne. You can help us wait."

Lou Anne flopped down like she was going to faint. "It's my fault," she moaned. "I wasn't paying attention, I was so mad at Andy. It's all my fault."

"She's gonna be okay, Lou Anne," Jemmie consoled her. "You didn't mean to make her sick."

Nana Grace came back with Artie on one hip and a pitcher of lemonade in her free hand. She took one look at Lou Anne sobbing and handed the baby to her. Lou Anne wrapped her arms around Artie and rocked him back and forth and dripped tears on the top of his head. Nana pulled a stack of paper cups out of the pocket of her apron. She filled and passed them out, then she dragged my old rocker over from behind the rose of Sharon bush.

And then we all sat. When Artie got fussy, we passed him around, but he always ended up back with Lou, who seemed to need a baby to hold.

Gradually, the heat went off the day. On the street a girl from Lou Anne's class went by on Rollerblades. "Hey, Lou! Guess who called me last night?"

"Not now, Steph, family emergency."

Steph skated backwards. "Sorry. I hope it works out." She turned and skated off, her long hair swinging side to side. Just before she disappeared around the corner she called, "It was Matt Logan!"

"Matt Logan!" Lou Anne exclaimed.

"He hot?" Jemmie asked Lou Anne.

"He sure is. He has blond hair and blue eyes and the cutest little butt." For a second Lou Anne was just Lou Anne, thinking about Matt Logan and his cute little butt. Then her eyes filled with tears again. She buried her face in Artie's neck.

The sun sank behind the live oak across the street. Nana Grace sang quietly. "I'm going back to see my father, I'm going back, no more to roam, I'm only crossing over Jordan, I'm only going over home." The chorus of night insects started up in the grass, and a breeze blew on my bare arms.

Lou Anne wiped her nose on the back of her hand. "What's that song about crossing Jordan mean?"

Nana didn't tell her that in the slave days it meant freedom, she just said, "Means goin' to a better place."

My sister sat very still and very straight. Tears spilled over her lower lids and down her cheeks. "You mean heaven, don't you?" Her voice was hoarse.

Nana Grace shook her head. "Not necessarily," she said. "That better place could be right here. This world could be heaven if we all did right."

"I know I'll do right from now on," Lou Anne said. "I'll take care of Missy so good...." Then she bit her lip, knowing she might never get another chance.

~

It was dark when the truck pulled into the yard.

We all crowded around the pickup, shoving our faces into the open windows. "Is she all right? You bring her home?" The only ones in there were Daddy and Jemmie's mother, sitting miles apart at opposite ends of the seat.

"Oh, no," Lou Anne wailed, "oh no," and she swayed as if she might fall.

Nana Grace grabbed her hand and held on hard.

Jemmie's mother climbed out first, looking at each of our faces so seriously I didn't want to hear what she had to say. "It's too early to know for sure," she said at last, "but it looks as if the baby will be all right." Lou Anne let out a moan and leaned against the truck.

"Your mother is staying with her overnight," Mrs. Lewis said. "She'll bring your sister home in a day or two."

"Oh, thank you, thank you!" Lou Anne put her arms around Mrs. Lewis and squeezed her in a big hug.

The driver's side door opened slowly. I've never seen Daddy look as tired as he did when he climbed out of that truck. His shoulders slumped. He came around our side of the truck with his baseball cap in his hand, then stopped in front of Mrs. Lewis and stood, running the bill of his cap back and forth between his thumb and index finger. He cleared his throat. "I want to thank you for tonight."

"That's quite all right," Mrs. Lewis answered.

"No, I owe you my baby's life." He held out his right hand.

Mrs. Lewis hesitated before taking it. After a quick handshake, they stood facing each other, not knowing what to do next.

"I don't know about y'all," said Nana Grace, "but I'm hungry. Let's go heat supper back up." The Lewises left. Lou Anne, Daddy, and me went in the house. I fixed us some supper, but Daddy didn't eat it. He just sat in the living room with the lights off.

He was still sitting like that when Lou Anne and I went up to bed.

CHAPTER SIXTEEN

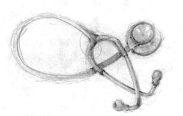

We Become Neighbors

Mama and Lou Anne spent the two days Missy was in the hospital in chairs beside her crib. When Daddy and I went over we offered to take their places but they wouldn't leave the hospital. The second afternoon Andy borrowed his father's car to go see Missy. Even though Lou Anne said it was all her fault, it seemed like he felt guilty too. He visited for a while, then because Mama was so tired, he brought her home to get some rest. As he walked her to the door I heard him ask, "Do you have a box of tissues, Mrs. Bodine? Lou Anne's cried her way through the first one." When he went back to the hospital just to bring Lou the fresh box of Kleenex, I thought, maybe Andy isn't that bad.

When Missy came home Lou Anne hung over the crib. "She seem a little droopy to you, Cass?"

And even though I thought she did, I said, "She's fine, Lou Anne. Perfect," because I didn't want Lou to feel bad anymore.

The first night the baby was home Daddy and Mama called Lou Anne into the living room. I could hear them talking to her about whether or not she was responsible enough to watch the baby. Aunt Claire had agreed to take Missy when school started, but Daddy thought we should start right now, considering what had happened. Lou Anne begged. She swore she'd never take Missy to the USA store again, that she'd cover her head if she took her outside, that she'd watch her every minute. As usual, Lou Anne convinced Mama. She had to work on Daddy longer but in the end he gave in.

It turned out Mama was right. Lou Anne became the perfect baby-sitter. I wouldn't have minded watching Missy sometimes, but Lou Anne wouldn't let me. She hung Missy around her neck like a great big piece of jewelry.

Jemmie and me started running together again, and I spent time over at her house like before. No one said we could, but no one said we couldn't either. What had happened with Missy had changed everything.

But things were hard in a different way. The grown-ups didn't know how to act. They were shy when they ran into each other. They smiled, but they couldn't think of anything to say.

"You watch," Nana Grace said the first Saturday after Missy came home from the hospital, "they gonna work it out." Jemmie, Nana Grace, and me were sitting on the Lewises' porch. Nana Grace was helping us make outfits for our porcelain dolls, showing us how to cut the parts out and sew them together. Jemmie's African queen doll was going to have a skirt pieced from a dozen different print fabrics. My doll, Jane, would have a blue satin outfit cut from an old dress of Lou's.

"Cass, would you thread this needle for me?" Nana Grace asked. "Seem like that bitty eye keeps winkin' shut."

I threaded it for her and handed it back.

"Now, this is how you do," she said. Her fingers worked quickly, the needle bobbing in and out of the fabric. "It's called a runnin' stitch. Get the idea?" She passed the fabric and needle back to me. "Just take yer time, do it right."

While we made careful running stitches, Nana Grace went back to chipping paint off the porch railings. Do it slow and do it right seemed to be her way to do everything. Little by little she was shining up Miss Liz's tired old house. She had painted most of the rooms and pulled the weeds out from underneath the rosebushes. Her gourd vines had grown so tall that one tendril had poked through the peek hole in the fence and grown down the Bodine side. There were two little gourds on it.

After a while I held up my doll dress with the needle sticking out like a quill. "I'm out of thread, Nana."

"Gracious, child, you got to leave a little to tie off with." She made me pick out a couple of inches of the stitches I'd worked so hard to make.

I heard a door slam and looked across the yard toward my house. Daddy had just come out. I waved at him. He tipped his ball cap, then walked off toward Mr. G.'s store to pick up cigarettes.

When he came back, he carried the bag with the carton of cigarettes in it into the house, but he came right back out with a propane torch and paint scraper and walked up to us. "How about letting me do that, Miss Grace?"

"Well, be my guest, Mr. Bodine. The rate I'm goin', I'll still be scrapin' rails come Judgment Day."

Daddy lit his torch and held the flame up to the railing. The paint bubbled and curled. With his free hand he scraped the curls away. It was faster than Nana Grace's scraping, but it smelled real bad. He sent us all inside so we wouldn't have to breath the fumes. We settled ourselves in Miss Liz's best parlor. The Lewises' table was a great big oval just like the one Miss Liz had had in there, only theirs wasn't rosewood. On theirs you could see dents where someone had pressed into it hard, writing on a piece of paper. Jemmie called it the homework table. We sat and sewed at the homework table and watched Daddy through the window as he inched along the rails.

When Jemmie's mother came into the room she stopped at the window. "We don't need him to do that. We could hire someone."

Nana Grace laughed softly. "Now, Leona, where we gonna get the money to hire someone? And anyway, that man won't rest 'til he pays you back some kind of way, so please, do me and my tired old hands a favor. Let him scrape the rails."

Mrs. Lewis saw that I was in the room and lowered her voice. "He doesn't owe me a thing. I would have done the same for anybody's baby."

"Heaven sake, would you give the man a chance? Try lookin' for the good in him. An' maybe," Nana said, wagging a finger at Jemmie's mother, "just maybe he'll do the same for you. That's the only way he's gonna learn you ain't the meanest black woman this side of Georgia."

Using the torch was quicker, but the work was still slow, and hot, and messy. When the sun swung around the house and beat on the porch, Daddy took off his ball cap. His bald patch was shiny with sweat. I was just going to ask Nana Grace for a glass of ice water to take out to him when we saw the screen door open onto the porch. Jemmie's mother had shoved it open with her hip. In each hand she had a sweating glass of icy lemonade. "You look hot, Mr. Bodine."

Daddy ran his bandanna over his bald spot, then down his neck. "Yes, ma'am, I am."

Mrs. Lewis handed him a glass, then she sat down on the top step with the second glass in her own hand. For a few minutes they just sat side by side with three feet of step between them. They sipped their lemonade and looked out into the yard.

"Been a dry summer," Daddy said at last.

"Yes, it has."

A warm wind blew a dust devil across the dry lawn.

"A hot one, too," she said.

After that they ran out of things to say so they just sat and stared straight ahead. They were so quiet I bet they could hear each other swallow.

$\sim$

Daddy spent that whole Saturday scraping railings. "No need to do it all at once," Nana Grace told him. "Ain't like Judgment Day's right around the corner." But he worked straight through the hottest part of the day and on into the evening.

Mama was canning tomatoes from Mrs. Henry's garden when he and I got home. "Your clothes are drenched," she told him. "You're working too hard. You're supposed to rest on the weekend."

"I'm going to pay that woman back." He took his cap off and slapped it against his thigh. "Even if it kills me."

The next day, after church, Nana Grace, Jemmie, and me were on the porch sewing again when he came back over. "Laura thought you might like some of the tomatoes she just put up." He set a couple of Mason jars on the porch rail, then picked up his torch and took out his cigarette lighter.

"Why, thank you, Mr. Bodine. I ain't had a home-stewed tomato since I don't remember when," Nana Grace said. "Why don't you come on in a minute, have a glass of tea with me and the girls before you get started."

Daddy puffed his cheeks and shifted from one foot to the other.

"No need to worry," she told him. "Dragon lady's off at the grocery store."

We all followed her back to the kitchen. "Now, ain't that the prettiest color?" she said, setting the jars of tomatoes on the windowsill. "Sit yourself down, Mr. Bodine, make yourself comfortable."

Daddy sat in a kitchen chair with his hat on his knee looking like someone had put ants down his back. He drank his iced tea quick and went straight to work.

He finished the rails, but I guess he still felt like he owed Mrs. Lewis, because after that he fixed a leaky faucet, and he figured out why the Lewises' washer got stuck on the spin cycle, and he wired a new porch light. Nana Grace thanked him after each project and told him what a wonder he was. But Jemmie's mother kept her distance.

Daddy kept his distance from her too. But he tuned right in to Nana Grace. He always seemed to know when she was doing something she shouldn't, like climbing onto the roof, or standing on the top rung of a ladder to nail loose shingles. "Now, Miss Grace," he'd say. "You come on down from up there."

One time he grabbed her by the waist when she was still a couple rungs from the bottom and lifted her off the ladder, with an "Upsy daisy," then he looked embarrassed. His ears were red as he scrambled up the ladder, his hammer swinging from the loop on his tool belt.

Then we all looked up at Daddy, who stood near the top of the ladder, a row of nails between his teeth, nailing loose shingles. It took one light tap to get the nail started, one heavy swing to drive it in. "You know, Cass," Nana Grace said as she held the ladder steady, "you get past all the vinegar, your daddy's a right sweet man."

I had to admit that, little by little, he was sweetening up, at least around Nana Grace. One evening, when he was fixing a squeak in her drier, he said, "Miss Grace, maybe I was hasty when I put up that fence." Then he stuck his head back inside the drier and began tightening something.

Jemmie and me glanced up from the drawings we were working on at the kitchen table and looked at Nana Grace. She pressed her lips together for a moment, then asked, "You live in Tallahassee long, Mr. Bodine?"

"All my life," his voice boomed from inside the drier.

"Then you must remember when the schools was separate."

While we were building the fence he had told me about how blacks had forced their way in where they weren't wanted, even though they had schools of their own. Now he pulled his head out of the drier and sat back on his heels. I could see his Adam's apple twitch as he swallowed. "Yeah. What about it?"

"When my Leona started school, you had to go fill out a special form sayin' you wanted your child to attend a white school. They made it hard. That's why there was so few at first; only four in the whole county the first year." I couldn't tell what Daddy was thinking but he looked as if he was really listening. "My Leona was too little to be in that first wave, but when the time come I filled out the form. There was more black children in white schools by then, but still, it wasn't easy sending her."

"Well, why did you?" he asked.

But Nana Grace didn't seem to hear. She was gazing over my father's head. "I remember bringin' her to the school that first mornin'. I had starched her white skirt, put ribbons in her hair. There wasn't a prettier child in that whole school." She twisted the end of the towel that hung over her shoulder. "When we got there white folks was droppin' their children off. Two of the men stepped right in front of Leona, called her a dirty nigger. Imagine sayin' a thing like that to a six-year-old child."

Daddy was staring at the floor like he was suddenly interested in the pattern on the linoleum.

"I was never so proud." Nana Grace said, lifting her chin, and I noticed that Jemmie lifted her chin too, listening to her grandmother. "Leona didn't cry. She hugged her lunch bag and she looked up at those men. 'Excuse me,' she said. But when she walked between them, one of the men spit on her dress."

"Wouldna happened if she'd stayed where she was s'posed to," Daddy mumbled.

Nana turned her pale brown eyes on him. "She went to school every day afraid. Afraid to use the little girls' room. Afraid of fights on the playground. Nights, gangs of white boys would come around the neighborhood and bomb our houses with water balloons."

"Water balloons? Sounds like they were just being kids."

"And their daddies would ride around in their pickups with their shotguns in plain view just to throw a scare into us. I was afraid for my child."

"Why'd you make her go, then?"

"Because she needed a decent education. We had fine black teachers in our schools, smart and hard workin', but the schools was broke down, meant to be second best." Nana Grace shook her head. "No sir, didn't matter how many folks stood in the way, my Leona was gonna get what she had comin'. A decent education." She clamped her jaw shut and turned away.

Jemmie and me shot each other glances across the table. It seemed as if things might go right back to the way they were before Missy got sick. We slipped up to Jemmie's room, worried, but in a few minutes we heard Daddy and Nana Grace laughing downstairs.

"I think your daddy likes Nana Grace," Jemmie said.

"He does. He said so at supper last night."

I didn't tell her what he said about her mother, though. "I don't have a thing against the woman," he had said. "She's just a little high and mighty for my taste. Looks at me like my neck's dirty."

I don't think she was worried about his neck, though. When Mrs. Lewis looked at him she saw a fence-building bigot. No matter how many things Daddy fixed, the fence was still there.

Luckily, Mama did better with Jemmie's mother. Mama discovered her soft spot. Mrs. Lewis wanted everyone to think she was a hard-shell kind of person, but as soon as she got around a baby she forgot all about that. It didn't matter what color the baby was either, or whether it was a boy or a girl. Jemmie's mother just loved babies. Mama did too.

The day Missy came home from the hospital, Mrs. Lewis and Jemmie stopped by. "Please, come in," Mama said.

Jemmie came in and sat down at the kitchen table with me, but her mother stood right inside the door with Artie on her hip. "I just came to check on the baby," she said, ignoring the chair Mama had pulled out for her, even when Jemmie whispered, "Sit down, Mom."

"Can I get you a sweet tea?" Mama said. "Missy's napping and Lou Anne's up there watching her sleep." Mama shook her head. "I just can't believe the change that's come over Lou Anne."

"You know," Jemmie's mother said, looking around, "the last time I was in a white woman's kitchen I was scrubbing the floor."

"You scrubbed floors?" Mama asked. "Now, whenever did you do that?"

"It was one of the jobs that got me through nursing school."

"I did maid work myself when Lou Anne was a baby. I absolutely hated it, didn't you?" Mama nudged the chair toward Mrs. Lewis.

She sat down. "It was pure torture."

"Tell the truth." Mama leaned toward her. "Have you ever met pickier women in your whole life?"

Mrs. Lewis shook her head. "Never. I never have. I had one woman who put on a white glove and ran it over every last thing just to make sure it was clean."

"I had one who made me clean her bathroom grout with a toothbrush on my hands and knees." Mama smiled at Artie and the baby reached for her. "Well, look at you. Aren't you the sweetest little thing?" She lifted the baby out of his mother's arms and set him on her own lap. "Such a nice big boy. Cass?" she called over her shoulder. "Be a sweetheart and get the Lewises some tea."

The next day, while Daddy was stripping the porch rails and Jemmie and me were at my house making ourselves some sandwiches, Mrs. Lewis came again. This time Missy was sitting up in her high chair slapping the tray with her palms.

"Where's that baby?" Jemmie's mother called through the screen door. Missy smiled a big toothless smile. "Where's that Missy Bodine?" This time Mrs. Lewis didn't wait for an invitation, she let herself in.

Mama took Artie, and Mrs. Lewis lifted Missy out of her chair. "Let's have a look at you," she said. She wore a stethoscope around her neck with the flat end in her shirt pocket. "Where's the teenager who's usually glued to this baby?"

"I had the afternoon off so I made her go out with her friend Carey."

We followed them to the living room, where Mrs. Lewis set the baby down on the sofa. Missy gave her a gummy grin. Mama watched while Mrs. Lewis examined the baby. "Let's get them some iced tea," I whispered to Jemmie.

"Good idea," she answered. "That'll keep 'em talking longer."

"Girl," Jemmie said as I dumped three heaping teaspoons of sugar into Mama's tea, "why don't you just pour a little tea in the sugar bowl and bring her that?"

"Mama likes it sweet," I said, stirring until the sugar disappeared.

"No joke." Her mother drank hers unsweetened with a chunk of lemon in it. I thought that their personalities were like their drinks, one sweet, one sour. But when we brought the glasses to the living room, our mothers were sitting on the sofa together, holding each other's babies, and Jemmie's mother was smiling like I'd never seen her smile before. "I swear, the first word Jemmie ever said was acrobat."

"Acrobat?" I hissed at Jemmie.

"My, three syllables." Mama nodded in approval. "Cass was no bigger than a minute when she learned how to use Seth's screwdriver. I remember, I was doing Lou Anne's hair and when I turned around she had the bottom of the screen door apart."

"No!"

"And Lou Anne won a savings bond for being the prettiest baby in Tallahassee."

"She's still a lovely girl."

"This is getting sickening," I whispered. "Let's go up to my room." The third step creaked as we ran up the stairs.

"So, this is your room." Jemmie looked around. "This pink isn't that pukey," she said. "Hey, somebody dropped this." She picked up the belt.

"That's on purpose." I flopped onto my bed. "It's the line between Lou Anne's half and mine."

Jemmie put it back down. "How come she gets the big half with the dresser and mirror in it?"

"'Cause she's oldest. She says that when she gets married I can have her side and Missy can take mine."

"When's she getting married?"

"Never, if Daddy has anything to say about it."

She plunked down on my bed too and crossed her legs. Since we had both read my magazines, I had cut them up and hung the pictures on the wall by my bed. We gazed up at the runners in their colorful running outfits, legs and arms pumping. "They don't look like they even touch the ground, do they?" she said.

"Maybe they don't. Maybe when you're a really, really good runner, gravity somehow doesn't apply to you anymore."

"That's gonna happen to us. We're gonna look just like this." She pointed at a runner with a red, white, and blue band around her forehead. The runner's arms were thrown back, her chest thrust forward to break the tape. Other runners were right behind her, but they were blurry, like they didn't matter. And they didn't. There wasn't a thing the blurry runners could do to stop her. In a heartbeat she'd hit the tape and win.

"Maybe it's the sneakers," I said. I had been thinking about sneakers a lot since I'd hung the pictures up. The sneakers in them were so cool. They all had special soles and built-in cushions for extra spring, and bright colors. I needed new sneakers bad. Mine had lost their bounce, and my feet had grown so much, I had to curl my toes to squeeze my feet inside, which didn't help my running. I had a couple of blisters. Luckily, so far Mama hadn't noticed. She would just worry and spend money she didn't have to get me another pair.

We turned and rested our backs against the wall, leaning on the famous runners in their famous shoes. Our legs were stretched straight out. Our soon-to-be famous feet were side by side.

"Someday there are gonna be running shoes with our names on 'em," Jemmie said, wiggling her bare toes. "The Jemmie Lewis is gonna have tongues of flame running down the sides. Smoke's gonna puff out the heels."

"They can make shoes that smoke?"

"Sure. Why not? How about yours?"

"The Cass Bodine will have stars, ones that glow in the dark, naturally."

"Naturally."

"And when I run they'll shower sparks just like a sparkler."

Jemmie thought about that. "Sparks'd be good, 'cept you might catch the grass on fire."

"They'd shoot a little water right after."

"I hope your sparking and squirting shoes fit better than the ones you have now," she said. "Yours are chewing your feet up bad."

"I guess my feet have grown over the summer. I'll get some new ones soon." As soon as we have the money, I said to myself, which wouldn't be soon at all.

"Cass? Jemmie?" Lou Anne was coming up the steps. "There you are. I brought you something." She had a piece of hot pink paper in her hand, which she held back for a second. "You two haven't been messing with my makeup kit or reading my diary, have you?"

"What would we want with your boring old diary?" I knew it was boring. I had read it before. Nothing was in it but stuff about boys and drawings of hairdos.

"What's that in your hand?" Jemmie asked.

"Oh, Mr. G. sent it. He said to give it to Chocolate Milk. He said you two would know who that was." The paper, folded neatly in quarters and stapled, landed on the bed between us. I pried the staple out and opened it up.

There were plenty of words on it, but one caught my eye: RACE. Jemmie snatched it out of my hand and read it to me, then I snatched it back and read it to her. Then she stood up on my bed. "This is gonna be you and me," she said, and she raised her arms and strained forward, like the runner in the sneaker ad, about to break the tape.

Lou Anne was baffled. "Are you two going to a dance?" She perked right up. "I'll do your makeup. Can I? You'll both look so cute."

In Training

When we read the small type, we found out that the race was a fund-raiser for sickle-cell anemia, which meant we had to do more than just run. We had to get sponsors, too.

Jemmie's mother got the doctors and nurses she worked with at the hospital to sponsor Jemmie. It wasn't hard. They all had money. And they all knew what sickle-cell anemia was.

I got Mr. G., who said the USA store would be proud to sponsor a team called Chocolate Milk, since he sold chocolate milk in pints and quarts. Mr. Barnett gave me two dollars, which was a big deal for him. He usually has to ask my mother if he can borrow bus money until his disability check comes in. Mrs. Henry gave me a couple of dollars, and so did Aunt Claire and Miss Johnette.

One afternoon Ben came to the door dripping wet. His brown hair was pushed-back wet.

"You been swimming?" I asked.

"Justin and me just sprayed ourselves with the hose. Hot, isn't it?"

I could see Justin waiting in the road, pedaling his bike in slow circles, drops falling off the hanging threads on his cutoffs. I remembered when Ben used to chase me with the hose or the two of us would run through the sprinkler on his front lawn.

"Come on, Ben," Justin called.

"Hold on, wouldya?" Ben shouted over his shoulder. Then he turned back around to me. "I hear you're collecting money for a race."

"How'd you hear about that?"

"Your mama told mine." He shoved his hand into his pocket and pulled out two dollars. "Here. I didn't want to forget." The bills were warm and wet from being in his pocket. "Say, what'd you do to your hair?"

"Lou gave me a haircut." I rolled my eyes.

"I'll say." When Ben was little he used to wear his hair bristly-short. I liked to rub his head. Now he looked like he was going to do the same to me, but he pulled his hand back at the last second and scratched his nose. "Good luck in the race."

"Thanks." I held the bills and watched him trot back to the street, leaving wet footprints on our concrete walk. He slowed for a second, looking down at the handprints in the cement, then turned and gave me a quick grin. The two of us had been playing in the yard the day Daddy poured the path. Our handprints were there, frozen in the cement. Our names had been scratched in with a stick: Ben and Cassy. Ben jumped on his bike and took off with Justin.

I put Ben's dollars with all the other money I'd collected and counted it at the kitchen table. "Eighteen dollars, Mama."

Mama took her coupon money jar down off the shelf and set it on the table. Each time she uses a coupon, she puts the amount of money she saved in that jar. She uses the money for things like new slipcovers for the sofa or a bath mat. Lately she'd been calling it her curtain money. She slid the jar toward me. "Count it, Cass. I bet there's close to thirty dollars in there, and it's all yours."

"But Mama, you need this for new curtains."

"Take it. It was your fast running that saved Missy's life."

When we spilled the money out and counted it, it came to forty-one dollars and twelve cents.

"I never thought it would be so much!" she said. She was proud to write her pledge on the line: Laura Bodine, $41.12.

After she gave me her curtain money, there was no way I could ask her for new running shoes. She'd already given me all the extra money she had in the world. I'd just have to run my fastest with my toes crinked. I made sure she didn't get a good look at my feet.

In the two weeks we had before the race, we ran even more than before. Jemmie kept that piece of pink paper with her all the time—in her pocket, even under her pillow when she went to bed.

She pulled it out when we were resting under the pecan tree and smoothed it out on the grass. While the Cortezes' dogs watched, she traced the squiggly map across the paper. "We got a couple of hills at the beginning. Not too bad. We should traverse them, no problem."

"But what about the sixteen year olds?" We would be competing in the twelve to sixteen year old category. Separate prizes for boys and girls. "You think we can beat them?" I asked, trying to adjust the laces of my sneakers to make the shoes feel bigger. "They're bound to be faster than us."

"No way." Jemmie lowered her voice. "They've got boobs, and boobs are just dead weight. They've gotta slow 'em down."

I wasn't so sure, but Jemmie insisted. "We're gonna win because of the boob factor, and because we've been working our buns off." She stood up and slid the paper back in her pocket. "Come on." Then we were off again, running. "We're in The Zone!" she yelled.

But we couldn't run all the time. We had to quit when it got too hot. That's when we missed *Jane Eyre*.

"Maybe Charlotte Bronte wrote another book that's just as good," I said once when we were sitting on my bed with nothing to do.

"That doesn't help us now. We won't be able to get it 'til we get back to school and go to the school library."

Lou Anne was across the room working on her cuticles. "You want to go to the public library?" she asked. "They have lots of books. Andy's got the car after work. We can run you down there, then drop you back home before we go to the movies."

"Andy? No way," Jemmie said.

But I was already digging around in my underwear drawer, looking for the library card I got on a once-a-month class visit. I wanted another book.

Andy didn't look thrilled when we got in the car, but he drove us over to the library. He and Lou Anne waited in the car while we went inside.

"Guess we better hurry," I said. I didn't want him giving my sister a hard time.

But Jemmie said, "He can wait." I could tell she was thinking about the way he humiliated her at the USA store. She took her time walking to the fiction section. "Bradley, Brenner, Brogan." She trailed a lazy finger along the *B*s.

I rushed ahead of her. "Here it is, Bronte." There was a copy of *Jane Eyre* in a mousy brown cover, nowhere near as nice as Miss Liz's. Next to it was another book with Bronte on the spine. I pulled it out. "Wrong Bronte." I was disappointed. "This one's named Emily."

I was about to shove it back but Jemmie took it out of my hand and read the jacket. "Says here Emily was Charlotte's sister." Then she read, "'Part mystery, part ghost tale, part realistic social portrait, this book gives new meaning to the word 'romantic.'" She turned it over and we stared at the title. "*Wuthering Heights*," we said together.

"What's Wuthering?" I asked.

Jemmie hugged the book. "We'll look it up." We checked our book out and Andy drove us home in record time.

We looked up wuthering first thing, but we couldn't find it.

"Maybe wuthering is the old way to spell withering," I said, so we used it that way. "These flowers you brought Miss Liz are wuthering bad," Jemmie would say.

"Well, they were the best I could find. The others were wuthered even worse."

~

The race was scheduled for the Saturday before school started. It would be a two-mile run around Myers Park. With the race less than a week away now, I had to admit that even with the boob factor, each of us had something to worry about. For me it was the shoes. With all the extra running we'd done lately, my shoes had rubbed my toes raw. For Jemmie it was the distance. Jemmie could've won any sprint against any sixteen year old, with or without boobs, but she wasn't good at pacing herself. She just went as fast as she could from the get go. If she did that in a two-mile race, she would poop out long before the end.

I put Band-Aids on my toes and did what I could for my sorry feet. Jemmie practiced conserving her energy for the final kick. She packed her pockets full of Foaming Fizz Powder packets for instant energy, and when we were both wuthering from thumping around and around the track, we'd pass a bag back and forth.

"It's like rocket fuel." She tipped her head back and shook the bag over her open mouth. "Between the boob factor and the fizz factor, we can't lose."

But would the boob factor and the fizz factor be enough? My toes, swollen and rubbed raw, had started to throb. The shoe factor was getting critical.

~

We sat on Jemmie's porch the evening before the race. I had my bare feet up on the railing, hoping the air would heal up my toes.

"Lord, child, what'd you do to your feet?" Nana Grace asked. "Your mama seen 'em?"

"No, ma'am."

"Leona?" she called. "Would you come out here and take a look at this child's feet?"

"They're okay." I hid my feet under the chair.

"What about her feet?" Mrs. Lewis came out drying a glass, the skin on her fingers puckered from washing dishes.

"Just take a look." And Nana Grace grabbed my ankle and held my foot out. "I don't see how the child's gonna run with her feet all blistered up."

Mrs. Lewis took my foot firmly by the heel and angled it so the porch light fell on it. "Cass, if you keep this up, you'll get a serious infection." She picked up my sneaker, then pulled back and wrinkled her nose. "This shoe should be taken out and shot."

"It's still good, honest. My parents wanted to get me a new pair, but I wouldn't let them. They're my lucky sneakers."

"Nonsense. Running fast doesn't have a thing to do with lucky sneakers. You're a good runner, Cass. But you won't be if you run much longer in these shoes." And she looked across to my house. The lights were out.

"They're all out at Wal-Mart," I said.

Mrs. Lewis thought a moment. "Cass, I'm going to sponsor you. Not with money, but with a pair of shoes. My daughter's already told me that you two plan to cross the finish line together. I have to make sure you can do that, now don't I?"

I should've said no. I should've wrapped my toes in Band-Aids and squeezed my feet into my old shoes, but I wanted us to win and I knew I would have a hard time getting through two miles with flames of pain shooting up my legs, much less winning.

And I wanted those new shoes as bad as Lou Anne wanted a seafoam blue wedding, so I made a mistake. I said okay.

As we trailed Mrs. Lewis through the mall, Jemmie whispered that she couldn't believe her mother was doing this. Like my mama, hers was always careful with every penny. When Mrs. Lewis told Jemmie she could get a pair too, we almost fell over.

We talked it over for a long time, but finally we picked identical shoes. Midnight blue with silver trim. The word COMET was printed on the heels. Jemmie pointed out the *C* and the *M* in Comet. "Chocolate Milk," she whispered, like our name was hidden there in secret code.

Jemmie kept walking up to the floor mirror to admire the way her Comets looked, but I didn't care how they looked. I just walked. I couldn't believe how good my feet felt. I could practically hear my toes let out a sigh as they wiggled inside the roomy new sneakers. The Comets were springy and practically lighter than air. I gave Jemmie a thumbs-up sign and she gave one back.

With the shoe factor on our side, we'd win this thing for sure.

The Shoe Factor

The next morning I got up before anyone else and showered. For the official race-morning breakfast, Jemmie had said we should eat something hearty, like a can of Chef Boyardee, but her mother said if we did that and then ran, we would probably throw up. "Eat light," she said. I was glad because my stomach was already in a knot.

I poured milk on my cold cereal and sat down at the kitchen table. Just chewing made me sweat. The weather was not salubrious. The air felt as hot and damp as Fran and Blackie's breath when they were panting in your face.

It was the wrong kind of weather for running—but it was the kind we usually got. When she was planning our futures, Jemmie would say, "When we're in the Olympics it had better be in some tropical country. That would sure give us an edge." Then she'd add that she hoped there'd be palm trees and sandy beaches, otherwise the Olympics would be just like running at Monroe Middle: hot and sticky.

I had put on my shorts and my T-shirt that said Tallahassee Cares. Lou Anne got it for volunteering at the children's shelter. Even though it was big I wore it because she guaranteed it would bring me luck. I put on my running shoes and laced them up. My feet seemed to hum like an electric current was passing through them. I propped them up on a chair so I could get a better look at my Comets.

"Big day, huh, String Bean?" As Daddy walked by he roughed up the back of my hair. Then he saw the shoes. "Where'd you get those?"

"Mrs. Lewis sponsored them."

"Sponsored?" He frowned. "What's that supposed to mean?"

"You know, like Mama gave her curtain money, and Ben gave me money from mowing lawns...you know, like that."

"How much did they cost?"

I took my feet down and tucked them under my chair. "They were on sale."

"I asked how much, Cass."

"Forty-eight dollars, but they were marked down from sixty-five."

Daddy's fist hit the table. The spoon in my cereal bowl jumped. "She did that on purpose. Just one more way to say she's better."

"Mrs. Lewis just wants me and Jemmie to have a good race."

He wasn't listening. "She thinks she's too good for us," he muttered. "She just has to rub my nose in it. You'll give those shoes back," he announced. "Your old ones'll do you fine."

"They won't do me fine, Daddy, I don't have them anymore. I threw them in the garbage can at the mall."

"Then you ain't gonna run." He turned and opened the refrigerator door like everything was all settled.

"But I have to run!" I shouted at his back.

He set the tub of margarine on the table. "Not in her forty-eight-dollar shoes, you don't."

"Please, Daddy!" For the first time in my life I did just like Lou Anne. Tears sprang from my eyes. I couldn't help it.

Mama shuffled into the kitchen in her slippers and housecoat. She looked back and forth between us. "Cass, honey, what's the matter?"

"Mrs. Lewis sponsored me some new shoes and now Daddy says I can't run."

"Mrs. Lewis *bought* her new shoes. Forty-eight dollars, Laura, and you know we can't pay that back just now. Cass threw the old ones out. If she can't run today, it's her own fault."

I could see Mama through my tears, soft and timid-looking in her pink robe. I knew that the thing she hated most was fighting with Daddy. She would slide things by him sometimes, or try to work out a compromise, but when it came to flat-out disagreeing with him, she kept her mouth shut. I knew there was no chance of a compromise here, no way to slide by. I would run in Mrs. Lewis's shoes or I wouldn't run at all.

But she didn't stick up for me. Instead she turned away and picked up the kettle, then scuffed over to the sink and turned on the water. My throat got all thick and I could feel myself shaking. Mama was a pink blur as she set the kettle on the stove and turned the burner on. I lurched up from my chair. I was set to run up to my room, when Mama said, "Sit down, Cass." Then she sat down herself and picked up Daddy's hand. "Let her keep the shoes, Seth."

He pulled his hand away, crossed his arms, and leaned back. "No way. I'm not going to owe Leona Lewis for a lousy pair of shoes. I'm not going to do it."

Mama took his hand back gently and held it in her lap. "The Lewises will be our neighbors for a long while, Seth. We'll pay them back sometime, but your daughter has a gift for running. Right now there's a race she needs to run, and she needs a pair of shoes to do it in." She looked into his eyes. "We owe Leona Lewis, but we owe Cass, too."

"And exactly what do we owe Cass?" He sounded impatient.

"A chance to shine," she said, holding his hand tightly with both of hers. "A chance to win."

He drummed the fingers of his free hand on the table. "All right," he said at last. "If it's that all-fired important, then all right. You better do us proud today, Cass." And he left the room.

I wanted to thank Mama, but my throat was all closed up. She gave me a hard hug and whispered, "Just do your best, honey. I'll be proud of you no matter what happens."

Go, Chocolate Milk! Go!

"G oodness," said Nana Grace, "I didn't know a body could bend like that." The runner in front of us was sitting in the grass with her legs straddled and her upper body bent forward. Her forehead touched the ground.

Jemmie and me put our palms against a tree and began stretching our calves. As we warmed up we looked around. Runners were everywhere, doing leg shakes, arm swings, and jogging in place. "It's just like the Boston Marathon out here," Jemmie said.

Our group, the twelve to sixteen year olds, would run first. There didn't seem to be too many twelve year olds getting ready, though, and the few girls who looked our age didn't act like they were serious about the race.

"What are you wearing the first day?" I heard one girl ask her friend. They sat on the grass, leaning back on their arms.

"I have these great new jeans and a really cute pink top," the other girl answered. The first girl said that she had great new jeans too, but her really cute top was blue.

Jemmie straightened up from a side bend. "If they don't warm up, those two are gonna be watching our really cute butts."

"Don't most of these girls look awful big to you?" Nana Grace's face was freckled with spots of light falling through the weave in her straw hat. "Bunch of giants."

"That's okay," Jemmie said. "We're small, but we're deadly."

It seemed like Jemmie got a kick out of coming up to the collarbones on most of the other runners, but I was scared. Suddenly I realized we couldn't win. Thinking we could win had been dumb. And if we didn't win, Daddy would stay mad about the shoes forever.

The Lewises had followed us over to the park in their pickup. The first thing my father did when we all climbed out was to thank Mrs. Lewis for the Comets, sounding all the time like he was accusing her of something, then he had shut his mouth. I watched him and Mama and Mrs. Lewis walk away, cutting across the park so they could get a good spot at the finish line. As they walked, Mama chatted with Mrs. Lewis in a pinched, high voice, trying to cover up the fact that Daddy wasn't talking at all.

If Lou Anne had been walking with them, she would've run her mouth until Daddy forgot to be mad and even Jemmie's mother would've had to smile, but she was home with Missy, who couldn't come because of the heat. "I wish I could see you run," she told me before we left. "I could do your makeup." When I told her I would just sweat it off, she looked disappointed. "At least you're wearing my lucky shirt," she said.

Jemmie and me sat on the ground and locked our ankles. Each time I sat back up I could see Nana Grace's skinny legs and the hem of her flower-print dress. Each time I lurched up, the flowers seemed to pulse and swim.

"Jemmie," I said, "I think I'm gonna puke."

"All you got's the jitters. You're up, adrenaline's pumping—you're ready, girl." She gave me a thumbs-up.

"No, I really think I'm gonna puke."

"Looks like you two gotta sign up over there." Nana Grace pointed out a folding table where other runners were lined up.

"Cass says she's gonna puke."

"You are not gonna puke." Nana Grace sounded stern. "You'll be fine."

"Honest, Nana, I don't think I can run."

Jemmie and me were both sitting up, our ankles still pressed together.

"If she can't run, I can't either." Jemmie said. "We're Chocolate Milk. We're a team."

"So, now both of you got Cass's stomachache." Nana Grace looked at me, then looked at Jemmie. "Didn't I hear a whole lotta talk about how you two was gonna win this race? Seems to me, you wanna win, you gotta run."

We joined the line.

"Names and ages?" the woman at the table asked when we reached the front.

Jemmie didn't say a thing. She just looked at me and waited.

The woman bounced her pencil point on her pad.

My stomach did a flip. "Jemmie Lewis and Cass Bodine," I said. "Twelve."

A Magic Marker squeaked across a pad. "You'll be 32 and 33. Good luck, girls." A second woman handed us sheets of paper with our numbers on them and a couple of safety pins.

"You got ants in your pants?" Nana Grace asked as she tried to pin the 32 on Jemmie. "You better hold still if you don't wanna get stuck." I held still as Nana Grace pinned my number to the front of my T-shirt.

The girls who were worried about their first-day-of-school outfits got their numbers. So did the muscled giants who were warming up all around us.

"Over there..." I whispered to Jemmie. "Does that girl look sixteen to you?" The girl who had been doing the straddle stretches now had a 40 pinned to her chest. She was wearing headphones with a small antenna on one side, so she wasn't hearing the shout of the hot dog vendor or the girls talking about their clothes. She was completely focused on getting ready to run, on finding The Zone. As she swung her arms, her shoulder muscles bunched. Her running shorts were blue nylon—the kind that weigh about two ounces and are supposed to make you a couple of milliseconds faster— and a narrow-strapped T-shirt with tiny holes all over it so she would stay cool. She didn't seem to notice the other runners at all.

Someone blew a whistle and everyone squeezed together behind the line painted on the road. Jemmie wanted to be up front, toeing that line, but we stayed at the back, which was part of my strategy. No need to get trampled. The girl with the headphones seemed to have the same strategy. She hung at the back, too, taking her own pulse. Next to her a young guy with a shaved head was shaking his arms out one last time.

A woman stood alone on the other side of the line. She held up her hand. "Just a couple of announcements before we start. First, I want to thank each and every one of you for raising money for sickle-cell anemia. And second, it's hot out here, so don't push yourselves too hard. We're here to have fun, right? In this race you're all winners."

"Yeah, yeah." Jemmie was jogging in place. Her feet were ready to go.

Me, I could have listened to announcements all day. I still thought I might barf. I concentrated on not barfing while the woman told us about the water station at mile one and the free ice cream for every runner at the end of the race, compliments of the local Kiwanis. Then she moved to the side so she wouldn't get trampled and raised the starter pistol over her head.

"On your mark…"

We all leaned forward.

"Get set…"

Jemmie looked like she wanted to pick up the boy in front of her and move him aside.

BAM!

The front of the pack took off, fanning out into the street. "Come on, Cass, let's perambulate." Jemmie slapped my butt, and we were off. A jolt traveled up my leg as I took the first step of the race. The road was harder than the dirt track at Monroe Middle.

"Go, Chocolate Milk!" shouted Nana Grace from the sideline, waving her straw hat. "Go!"

At first it was chaos. Everyone ran with their arms pulled in tight, dodging elbows and sneakers. "Just like the Y," Jemmie yelled.

In about a minute, though, things began to sort themselves out. The girls who were worried about their school clothes were right in front of us. They began to puff immediately. "Is two miles real long?" one asked the other. I could see that the front of the pack was peeling away, leaving the slower runners behind, and we were bottled up behind two of the slowest.

Jemmie always told me that if I didn't hurry up she was going to run up my back and down my front. The girls in front of us would be wearing our footprints if they didn't pick it up.

"Come on, Cass, let's traverse with a little more hustle." We ran right up to the girls, then parted, veered around them, and came back together.

The serious runners had pulled away, but we caught up with them. That's when we got our first look at the real competition. Most of the runners were huge. I felt like we were running in heavy traffic.

Surprisingly, out ahead of the pack were a couple of small runners, two boys I knew from Monroe Middle, Mark and Jerome. Mark turned and ran backwards for a few steps, waving us on with his arms. "Come on, people, keep up," he called, then he turned and wiggled his butt.

"What a jerk," Jemmie said. "Let's show him, Cass."

I held her back. "Remember, Jemmie, we've gotta pace ourselves. Look at number 40."

Number 40 was at the middle of the pack, running steady. She didn't pay any attention to Mark and his wiggling butt. In fact, she didn't seem to notice the other runners at all. She lifted her knees and arms high, but not too high. She looked like she could run for hours. We matched our pace to 40's.

Some of the runners were beginning to puff and sweat. If they usually ran indoors, they probably felt like they were running through wet cement. But running and heat were just business as usual for Jemmie and me.

We ran by the tennis courts where the players stood at the fence watching the race pass. Jemmie waved. Two men lifted their rackets.

There were still lots of pumping legs and arms in front of us, but it seemed that by keeping pace with 40 we were gradually pulling toward the front. Mark, the kid who had told us to keep up, was barely running now. Jemmie and me scissored around him. "Come on," Jemmie called over her shoulder, "keep up." She wiggled her butt at him.

I tried to concentrate on my own rhythm. That's the secret of running a long distance; paying attention to what your body is doing. Mine was doing okay. Sure, I was hot, I could feel a trickle of sweat like a cold finger running down my spine, and the shock of racing on pavement was making my legs hum, but my wind was still good. Best of all, I didn't want to barf anymore.

"Can we pick it up a little, Cass? Please?"

I could practically hear Jemmie's engine revving.

"We could be out of here," she said. "We could leave these guys in the dust."

I shook my head no. The other runners could've left us in the dust just as easily. They didn't because it would be a dumb thing to do. Who cares who's out ahead at the first half mile?

Some of the guys had pulled so far ahead that they were going up the next hill when we were still going down the first. A black guy and a white one were in the lead, running shoulder to shoulder. I wondered if they were friends like Jemmie and me, planning on crossing the line together. Then I saw the white guy pull ahead without even glancing back.

Most of the runners around us slowed on the uphill stretch, but not 40, and not Chocolate Milk. We passed a few more runners. There were a couple dozen in our pack. Jemmie and me were the only young ones left. Mark and Jerome had dropped out on the first hill. The two girls were way behind us. By now they were probably sitting in the shade discussing the cute shoes they were going to wear with their jeans and cute tops.

Near the mile, little tables were set up along the sidelines. Arms reached out offering water in paper cups. Runners took them without breaking stride and drank as they ran. Some took a gulp or two, then emptied the rest over their heads. I got mine. The water was warm, but it tasted really good. I could've drunk a gallon, but I saved some to pour over my head to see what it was like. Just like the marathoners I'd seen on TV, I held the cup over my head and dumped it. It didn't work out so well. It dripped into my eyes and for a second I couldn't see a thing. I ran right into 40's back.

"Watch where you're going, little girl." She glared over her shoulder and moved away from us.

"Who're you calling little girl?" Jemmie shouted at her back.

After the water break we hit a straight stretch. Way out ahead I could see three guys running. They would beat everyone in our pack. It didn't matter, though. All the girls—our competition—were in the group with us. The lead girl was no more than ten feet ahead. We could've caught up to her easy, but we held the pace.

I could hear the rattle of the beads Nana Grace had used to finish off Jemmie's jillions of braids. We were in the serious part of the race now. About ten of us were running together. Unless the heat caused someone to cramp, it looked as though our group would all cross the finish line. The only thing left to figure out was the order in which we'd do it.

As we ran I discovered that in the middle of the race there was a quiet spot. At first I had been all jitters, and I knew that at the end my muscles would be screaming. But in the middle there was a quiet part when the rhythm of running took over. Maybe I was finally in The Zone. I glanced over at Jemmie.

She didn't seem to know about the quiet spot. She wanted action. She signaled me that we should pull up a little. I shook my head. We were fine right where we were; not at the front, not at the back, our legs keeping up a steady rhythm.

"I could run like this forever, Jemmie," I said, glancing at number 40. She looked like she would run forever too.

"Not me," said Jemmie. "I want this race over, with us wearing ribbons around our necks. Girl, let's kick this thing into gear and go."

I could see that she was shiny with sweat, panting a little. "Too much race left for that," I said. For a time we all ran in formation.

No spectators were watching this part of the race. Anyone who hadn't cheered the runners when the starter pistol fired was waiting to cheer at the finish line. "This is kind of boring," Jemmie said. I saw a few heads turn, looking at Jemmie. "I'd fall asleep running a marathon."

I realized then that Chocolate Milk might not always run side by side. Jemmie was a sudden kind of person, a sprinter. Like Jemmie, a sprint is excitement from start to finish. I'm slower and steadier. I like the long hauls, when the only thing I have to pay attention to is keeping my breathing smooth and even.

Jemmie picked up the pace and I let her, at least until we passed 40, which was enough to satisfy her for a while.

"Time for the fizz factor." Jemmie pulled a packet of Foaming Fizz Powder out of her pocket, tore the top with her teeth, then offered it to me. I shook a little onto my tongue, where it foamed and fizzed. It seemed as impatient as Jemmie. I was passing it back to her when number 40 decided it was time to move up a little. Arms pumping, she ran right between us. The candy packet flew out of my hand, showering shiny crystals on the ground. "Girl!" Jemmie yelled. "I'm getting tired of you."

Number 40 didn't seem to hear a thing, and she didn't look back.

"That girl's a running machine," I said.

"Yeah, well it's time for us to show her what we got under the hood."

"Not yet, Jemmie…soon." Running alone I might've tried, but Jemmie was panting, and she was sweaty. I was afraid she'd overheat.

And she wasn't the only one suffering. Some of the other runners were flushed like Missy was the day she got the heat prostration. The girl beside us kept swiping at her forehead with her wristband. I could see sweat dribbling off the tips of another runner's short hair. Out ahead, number 40 looked cool and dry. She was lifting her heels exactly as high as she had at the start, and she still looked like she could go forever.

Suddenly, one of the runners veered off the road and sat down hard in the grass. She pulled her knees up and put her head on them. We all looked over at the girl who had been running beside her. "Dizzy," she explained.

"Man, what jerk came up with the bright idea of running in August, anyway?" asked another girl.

We began to see a few people scattered along the side of the road ahead of us. The finish line was coming up.

"What do you say, Cass?" Jemmie asked. "Time to move?"

"Let's get ahead of the rest, and just behind 40."

"Cass…I want to show 40 my back. I want to wuther that girl."

"First, let's get away from the pack."

We picked up the pace, but we weren't the only ones who wanted to show their backs to 40. The whole pack was running faster now, pounding for the finish line.

"Oh, the heck with it," Jemmie said, "let's perambulate." And she began to run full-out.

It was too early.

We still had a ways to go, including the last uphill stretch, but I would have had to nail Jemmie's Comets down to keep her from going.

So I went with her. Even though I thought we'd run out of steam before we got to the line, I went. After all, we were Chocolate Milk. Whether we streaked across the line first, or dragged across it dead last, we would do it together.

I didn't look back, but I knew we had pulled away from the pack because the sound of their footfalls grew quieter.

"We got it now!" Jemmie said as we pulled ahead of number 40. But I knew we didn't, not with that running machine so close behind.

The crowd along the edge of the road was getting thicker. I picked out Ben shading his eyes with his hand. "There she is!" he yelled.

I could hear the cheers, Daddy's loudest of all. I could see Mama hugging everyone around her, even Jemmie's mom. Maybe if it was Jemmie Lewis and Cass Bodine in a photo finish, our parents would be so proud they would forget all the hard feelings and be friends. Stretched across the road was a Day-Glo pink ribbon. The boys' leaders were headed right for it. One of them would break it long before we got there. Still, I could almost feel it stretch against my chest, then snap.

But 40 was still running right behind us, and she was getting closer. She sounded like she was about to step on the backs of our Comets.

"Pick it up, Cass, pick it up!" Daddy yelled.

I could've picked it up a little, but I could hear Jemmie's breathing, so loud it sounded like it was tearing her chest. Her lips were pulled back. We were running about three feet apart, but I moved in closer to let her know we were together no matter what, and that's when 40 made her move.

Like a blue flash, 40 cut between us. Jemmie told me later that she had heard 40 pulling up, had even heard the sound of her breathing. When she did, Jemmie tried to run faster, but couldn't. She had nothing left. Still, she strained forward as if wanting it so badly could get her there first. That's when 40's shoulder clipped hers. It was just a light brush, Jemmie said. Later, when she got over being mad, she had to admit that 40 probably hadn't even noticed.

At that moment one of the guys broke the tape, so there was a huge cheer just as Jemmie fell. Every braid stood out, every bead flashed as she pinwheeled on a twisted ankle, and the crowd roared. It happened in a heartbeat. One second she was with me, the next she was gone. I looked back over my shoulder. As she fell, she threw her arms out. Her body shook with the jolt of hitting the road, and her hands scraped across the pavement. The distance between us was getting wider and wider and I was still running.

Daddy yelled, "Don't look back, Cass! Run!"

Number 40 was ahead of me, but not by much. It seemed like she'd used her last kick just getting ahead of us.

"Come on, Cass!" Daddy yelled again.

If I could catch up with 40 I would be the winner all by myself.

Ben was jumping up and down yelling, "You can do it, Cass!"

But I couldn't do it, I couldn't leave Jemmie behind, so I turned back.

"Are you crazy, Cass?" Daddy yelled.

"You crazy, girl?" Jemmie was kneeling on the road. She waved me away. "Go on, get outta here." Tears streaked her cheeks. Both palms were bleeding. "Go!"

"Not without you," I said. So I wouldn't touch her hurt hand I grabbed her arm and slung it around my neck. "Come on, let's go." I lifted her up.

There was a cheer. Number 40 had crossed the line.

"You could've won it, Cass," Jemmie said as we hobbled along. "You could've."

The other runners in the pack passed us. There were scattered cheers as they crossed the line. I thought the audience would wander away, but they didn't. They started calling out to us, "Come on thirty-two, come on thirty-three, you can do it!"

Jemmie had taken too hard a fall to hurry. Even with most of her weight on me she could still barely hobble. "Come on!" the crowd shouted. When we stumbled across the line I was practically carrying her, but everyone was cheering, even Daddy. When I looked at Ben he grinned and gave me a wink.

A woman pointed a camera at us and snapped our picture, although I couldn't see why. We were the losers.

She whipped out a small pad. "Can I get your names, girls?"

Jemmie lifted her head up. "Chocolate Milk," she said.

"Excuse me...chocolate milk?"

"That's right," I said. "We're a team. Jemmie Lewis and Cass Bodine: Chocolate Milk."

The Winners

Wouldya look at this," Daddy whooped. "Cass made the front page." He pushed his coffee cup and plate of eggs to one side and spread out the newspaper.

Mama, with the coffeepot in one hand, leaned over Daddy's shoulder and read the caption. "Runners Jemmie Lewis and Cass Bodine, also known as Chocolate Milk, cross the finish line at the Annual Sickle-Cell Anemia Fun Run."

I couldn't believe it. There we were in the paper, Jemmie and me, our arms around each other's necks.

Lou Anne looked over my shoulder. "Oh, Cass, I told you you should've let me do your makeup. You look like you don't have any eyelashes."

"Lou Anne," Mama said, "it was a race, not a beauty pageant." She went to the catch-all drawer to get the scissors.

Lou Anne pouted. "It never hurts to look good."

But Mama wasn't listening. She was cutting out our picture and saying she didn't remember the last time she felt so proud.

Mr. G. cut us out too, and he didn't say one thing about my eyelashes. In fact he said, "You two young ladies look magnificently lovely," and then he taped our picture to the cooler door. "Jemmie, Cass, in your honor I am putting chocolate milk—which I sell in pints and quarts—on special, two for the price of one, this week only."

At home, Mama and Mrs. Lewis stuck the pictures on our refrigerator doors. Mrs. Henry called me to say that her church friends were all saving copies. "You two will want to show them to your children someday," she said.

~

Jemmie's ankle was still wrapped when we walked to school Monday morning. "Too bad summer's over," she said, limping a little. She was wearing a new outfit her mother had bought her at the mall and a pair of lucky shooting star earrings. I had on a new shirt. We both wore our Comets. Jemmie kicked a rock with her good foot as she walked along, and kept her eyes down.

"What's the matter?" I asked.

She shrugged and gave the rock another kick. "New school. New kids."

"Hey, it's no big deal." But I was worried too. I didn't know how other kids would treat us. As we walked up to the school yard we could see the kids waiting outside. It had never bothered me before, but now I couldn't help but notice that black kids and white kids were hanging around in two separate bunches.

"Cass! Jemmie!" Ben broke away from the boys he was standing with. "I saw your picture in the paper." A group of girls that had been watching Ben like they'd been starving to see him all summer followed him. "That was some race you two ran," he said.

"Thanks," Jemmie said. "Listen, I'd still like to shoot hoops with you sometime if you think you're up to it."

"How about after school today?" When Ben flicked one of Jemmie's earrings with his finger the girls came toward us in a clump.

"Hi, Cass, who's your friend?" they all asked.

If Jemmie had the Ben Floyd seal of approval, they were ready to meet her.

It turned out that Jemmie and me had four of the same classes. We sat together for those. Mitch Cooper called Jemmie my black shadow. I told him to stuff it. Jemmie introduced me to Janella and Nakita, a couple of the black girls from one of the classes she took without me. I'd been in school with them all my life but had never talked to them much before. Janella said that she'd like to run with us sometime after school.

∼

"School's okay," Jemmie told Nana Grace after the first week.

"I told you it'd be fine. Would you get me a couple more apples out of the icebox, child?" It was Saturday afternoon and we were helping Nana Grace make a pie. The Bodines and the Lewises were going to be eating supper together.

"You know," Jemmie said, pausing to look at our picture before she opened the refrigerator door, "sometimes I forget we didn't win that race."

Nana Grace stopped peeling the apple she had in her hand. "What you mean you didn't win?"

"We crossed the line almost in last place, Nana."

"Maybe in the Fun Run you did. That don't matter. Y'all crossed the Bodine-Lewis line first. Now that is really somethin'."

We put the pie in the oven and I went back to my house to make macaroni salad. When I walked in Mama was making a Jello concoction with grapes and grated carrots in it.

"Where's Daddy?"

Mama bit her lip and looked away. "Still out in the garage," she said. He had been in there banging things together when I left for Jemmie's. Now there was a crash. "He's rearranging boxes," Mama said.

"Sounds more like he's throwing things."

Mama set down the carrot she was grating and wiped her hands. "Cass, he's a little upset about this supper. I didn't ask him before I told Jemmie's mother we'd come."

"He doesn't want to go?"

"It's not that, exactly. He's just a little uncomfortable with it."

"What do you mean, uncomfortable?" Adults never said what they meant unless it was good. "He doesn't want to eat with the Lewises because they're black, right?"

Mama opened her mouth, then closed it again and stared at me hard. "That's right. It isn't easy for him to change, Cass. But he is trying."

Daddy stuck his head in the kitchen. "Laura," he said, "I don't know where we got all this crap, but about half of it's going out to the curb." Then he went back to the garage to make more noise.

I thought about Nana Grace, cooking up a storm next door. I thought about all the food that would get cold and all the hard feelings if Daddy got stubborn. "He will go with us, won't he?" I whispered.

~

"Yoo-hoo," Mama called through the Lewises' screen door. She stood on the front porch holding a jiggly Jello ring on a platter against one hip and Missy on the other.

"I'll get it, Mom." Jemmie ran to the door and opened it. Lou Anne and I followed Mama in.

Jemmie wore a white dress and sandals and her braids were studded with silver beads. "You didn't tell me you were getting dressed up," I whispered.

"Nana made me. She said it was a special occasion."

Jemmie's mother walked over to the door and looked out. Daddy was still outside. He was carrying Missy's high chair. You would've thought it weighed a ton, he was moving so slow.

"Care to join us, Mr. Bodine?" She had Artie on her hip but she pushed the door open with her free hand.

"Seth?" Mama said.

Daddy took his ball cap off and came inside.

Missy was reaching out for Mrs. Lewis.

"Well now, Laura," Mrs. Lewis said, "you can just pass that sweet baby to me." And like they always did at our house, they traded babies.

Lou Anne stood clutching the bowl of bread and butter pickles and the basket of biscuits she had carried over, looking around with her mouth hanging open.

Mama whispered, "Quit staring, Lou Anne."

"Excuse me," Lou Anne said to Mrs. Lewis. "It's just that I've never been inside an African-American home before."

Mrs. Lewis stopped cooing at Missy. "Oh, and how do you like it?"

There was a tense silence and I thought, Don't blow it, Lou Anne, please don't blow it.

Everyone held their breath as Lou Anne looked around one more time. "It's cute!"

Jemmie rolled her eyes. Mrs. Lewis laughed.

"I sure hope y'all brought your appetites," Nana Grace said, stepping out of the kitchen carrying a platter of fried chicken.

She led the parade to the table in Miss Liz's best parlor. Mrs. Lewis sat at the head of the table, where Miss Liz used to sit at the doll tea parties. Daddy sat at the foot. The rest of us sat along the sides in the doll's places. I was next to Jemmie.

Nana Grace looked at Daddy. "Would you ask the blessin', Mr. Bodine?"

We bowed our heads. I guess I expected him to say the usual blessing, "Thank you Lord for food and family." He cleared his throat. There was a long pause, then he said, "Thank you Lord for food and friends." Everyone looked up.

"A-men," said Nana Grace loudly.

"A-men," we all said.

"Chicken, Miss Grace?" Daddy held the platter out.

"Thank you, Mr. Bodine." Nana Grace helped herself to some of the chicken she'd just made.

Lou Anne passed the biscuits.

Jemmie kept a straight face as she pinched me under the table. I kept a straight face as I flicked her leg with my napkin.

Mama and Mrs. Lewis put little piles of food in front of Missy and Artie, which the babies mushed around on their high chair trays.

Jemmie used up half of the sausage gravy smothering her biscuits.

Nana Grace watched as Daddy piled his plate high with food. "It's good to see a man with an appetite," she said.

"A snack like this is good as a meal," he joked.

After that the only sound was the clink of silverware as we all dug into the first-ever Bodine-Lewis potluck supper.